Every Day and All the Time

Every Day and All the Time

SIS DEANS

Henry Holt and Company / New York

Writing a book takes the help and encouragement of many people. I would like to thank adolescent school psychologist Jayne Boulos for reading the manuscript and sharing her expertise. To all the orthopedic surgeons I work with in the OR at Mercy Hospital, thank you for your input regarding Emily's fracture and course of treatment, especially Dr. Hanley and Dr. Khun. To writers John Cofran and Wanda Poore Whitten, thank you for your friendship and for sharing your talent. To my editor at Henry Holt, Reka Simonsen—you're the best and I'm glad you're on my team. To Terry Evans-Zaroff, my copy editor, thanks for covering all the bases and checking out the details. To my agent, Upton Brady, thanks for seeing in me something others didn't. To my mother—my hero and greatest fan—thank you for always being in my corner. To my husband, John, and our three girls, Jessie, Rachel, and Emma—your love is my inspiration.

Henry Holt and Company, LLC, *Publishers since 1866*
115 West 18th Street, New York, New York 10011
www.henryholt.com

Henry Holt is a registered trademark of Henry Holt and Company, LLC

Distributed in Canada by H. B. Fenn and Company Ltd.

Library of Congress Cataloging-in-Publication Data
Deans, Sis Boulos. Every day and all the time / Sis Deans.
p. cm.
Summary: Eleven-year-old Emily, still reeling from the car accident that took her older brother's life and badly injured her, uses psychotherapy and ballet dancing to cope with her parents' decision to sell their house—the only place she can still feel and talk to her brother.
[1. Grief—Fiction. 2. Brothers and sisters—Fiction. 3. Ballet dancing—Fiction. 4. Psychotherapy—Fiction. 5. Maine—Fiction.] I. Title.
PZ7.D3514Ev 2003 [Fic]—dc21 2002038893

ISBN 0-8050-7337-X / First Edition—2003
Designed by Martha Rago
Printed in the United States of America on acid-free paper. ∞
1 3 5 7 9 10 8 6 4 2

For my brother Jon,

whose laughter I still hear
in quiet moments

—S. D.

Every Day and All the Time

one

THROUGH THE WINDOW of Dr. Radke's office, eleven-year-old Emily could see a maple tree, its fiery leaves waving at her like hands in the autumn breeze. Come outside, they seemed to beckon, come dance in the wind with us. She squinted just enough to blur the colors, and unexpectedly the earliest of all her memories surfaced. She closed her eyes and held on to that clear picture of her brother's hand holding out the flower for her to take. Yellow and orange, the colors of sun and fire, the colors of an Indian paintbrush, and her own tiny fingers reaching for the green stem.

The image only lasted a moment; that's all she ever saw—Jon's hand holding out the flower, and hers reaching for it. Even before she opened her eyes and picked up an orange crayon, the warm feeling the memory always brought was fading. Without thinking, she began to draw flowers along the cellar windows in her picture, and once again the fear of what she'd overheard the night before hit her like an icy ocean wave.

"It's not you, Michael," her mother had said. "It's this house. I don't want to come home to it anymore. Everywhere I look, I . . ."

"Maybe you're right," her father had replied. "Maybe moving would be the best thing for all of us."

Emily bore down so hard on the paper that the tip of the crayon began to crumble. We can't move, she thought. What would happen to Jon if we did? That scary question had kept her up most of the night and followed her around all day.

She glanced about the empty room, wondering what was taking Dr. Radke so long. She wanted to get this over with so she could go home. She didn't know why she had to come here in the first place. Just because she was a kid, all the grownups thought she "needed someone to talk to," but the truth was, she didn't want to talk about her brother's death at all. Neither did her mother or father, but no one was making them go to a psychologist every Monday afternoon.

Just then Dr. Radke glided into the room, her long slender hands gesturing in the air as she apologized. "I'm sorry to have kept you waiting, Emily. Minor emergency on the home front."

"That's okay," Emily told her, then eagerly added, "I can come back another day if you need to go home."

The doctor smiled at her and slipped into the leather chair behind the desk. "That's very kind of you," she said, "but it won't be necessary. It was just a car-pool problem with my son, who plays soccer. Nothing a few phone calls couldn't fix. You know what it's like having a mother who works."

Emily knew, all right; her mother was a surgeon. Her parents' fight last night had started over her mother working too much, her father shouting, "The only reason you keep covering everyone at the hospital is because it gives you the perfect excuse not to be home."

"Right?" asked the doctor.

"Yeah," Emily answered, "I know what you mean. My mom's always taking someone's appendix out in the middle of the night."

"How *is* your mother?"

I need to work right now or I'll go crazy, that's what her mom had told her dad last night. "Good," said Emily. "Working a lot."

"And what about you, Emily? How are you doing?"

I'm tired and my leg hurts and I need to go home and tell my brother our parents are going to sell the house we've lived in all of our lives. "Fine, thank you."

"Is there anything you'd like to tell me before we get started?"

Emily looked past the doctor to the window and the fiery-colored leaves. She'd wanted to tell Jon last night, but the only way to reach the cellar was through the kitchen, and her parents would have caught her. Then, this morning, she'd overslept and there wasn't any time. She'd gotten up so late she'd missed the bus, and her father had had to give her a ride to school. Not that she minded. She hated riding the bus—it scared her.

Although Jon would never sit with her, he'd always been there to protect her. All the kids had liked him, and because they knew he'd pound anyone who dared to give her any grief, there was only one time that anyone had. When she was in kindergarten, a fourth-grader named Dan Maxwell had pulled her braid hard enough to make her cry, and Jon, who was only in second but big for his age, went mental. By the time the driver had a chance to stop the bus safely, Dan Maxwell had a torn shirt, a fat lip, and a bloody nose, and her brother had a reputation: Jon Racine will beat the crap out of anyone who messes with his little sister.

"Emily?"

She looked back at the doctor, who had a long, pretty neck like a swan. "I'm sorry," she told her. "I forgot the question. I must have been having a 'senior moment,' like my gram likes to say."

Dr. Radke laughed. "Don't worry about it, it wasn't that important. Besides, I know it must be hard for you, being here on such a beautiful afternoon, when you could be outside playing with your friends."

He can't play outside anymore, thought Emily, then glanced down at the picture she'd been drawing. The house and yard were outlined in black, but the flowers along the cellar windows were bright orange with green stems.

"I know it's hard for me," confessed Dr. Radke, turning slightly in her chair. "One of the reasons I moved back to Maine was because it has four seasons—and fall's always been my favorite. Speaking of which, how's school going?"

Emily put down the crayon and considered the question. The first week of school had been the hardest for her. All those whispers and stares. All those teachers saying, "I'm sorry," or

"It's good to have you back," or "How are you and your family doing?" She hated saying thank you when people said they were sorry about her brother's death; it was like taking a present from them that she didn't want. But what else was she supposed to say—don't worry, he's still living in the cellar?

Rolling the crayon with her finger, she told Dr. Radke, "We've hardly had any homework, and my teacher's not very organized, but other than that, things are going well." I haven't had to say thank you for almost three weeks.

"I'm glad to hear that," said the doctor; then she looked at Emily expectantly, as if waiting for more.

Unsure of what to say, Emily glanced around the nicely decorated office to buy herself some time. She was a listener, had never been a talker; her brother had always done that for her. Whenever the ice-cream truck came through their neighborhood, he always ordered for her. He'd talk to anyone, including strangers—he could even make strict teachers laugh. Her mother liked to tell people, "Jon's my entertainer, and Emily's my shy one," and that was the truth. Emily would rather go without an ice cream than order one herself. She only talked when it was necessary or when she had something important to say. Now, as she searched for something to tell Dr. Radke, a painting on the mauve-colored wall caught her attention. It was a splattering of soft Easter colors against a white canvas, and its thin black frame needed to be straightened. Although Emily didn't like the painting, it bothered her that it was crooked. "Jessie Perkins' mother took her to the Monet exhibition at the Portland Museum of Art," she finally said.

"Do you like Monet?"

Emily nodded. "He's my favorite painter. I like his early work the best."

"You should ask your parents to take you, then," Dr. Radke suggested.

"The show's over," said Emily. "It was here when they were doing all that stuff to my leg, so I couldn't go."

"That's a shame," said the doctor. "You know, art's such a good way for people to express their feelings. I can tell a lot from the pictures you've drawn for me. May I look at the one you did today?"

Emily pushed the drawing across the desk, then shifted in her chair and took a quick peek at her left leg to make sure her wind-pants hadn't ridden up. She didn't want anyone to see those ugly scars. Her mother had called the horrible contraption that had held her bones in place while they'd healed an external fixitor. To Emily it had looked like something out of a scary movie. It reminded her of the bolts in Frankenstein's head. The first time she was awake enough to watch her orthopedic surgeon change the gauzy white dressing that was wrapped around the metal frame, she'd passed right out. One look at all those pins sticking out of her leg and the black rods that connected them with metal clips and nuts was too much for her. She'd never even noticed the open wound that, in another operation, had been covered with a skin graft taken from her bottom. All she'd remembered before fainting was seeing a leg skewered like a piece of barbecued chicken, and then realizing it was hers.

Tilting the picture so Emily could see it, too, Dr. Radke asked in that kind, lullaby voice of hers, "Would you like to share this with me?"

Emily looked down at the drawing. If she'd had a ruler she could have done a better job, could have made the black windows straighter. "It's my house," she said, and then pointed at one of the windows. "This is my room, and that one used to be Jon's." Her finger slid down the paper until it rested on one of the flowers by the cellar window. And this is where he lives now, she thought to herself, but that was something she wasn't about to "share" with Dr. Radke, who seemed to be in love with that word.

The doctor leaned closer, and Emily caught a faint scent of lilies. "All those trees, and a pool," said Dr. Radke. "Looks like a house I'd want to live in."

"It's not for sale," Emily told her emphatically.

"Oh, don't worry, I already own a house," said the doctor, then added with a chuckle, "Or you could say it owns me. It's a beautiful old house, but I'm always having to have something fixed. Last summer, the roof and gutters; this week, the water heater."

Emily figured her house must be pretty old, too, because her father was always trying to fix something, which meant the plumber or the electrician or the pool guy then had to come and fix it right.

"If I had to do it all over again, I'd buy land and build," said Dr. Radke.

"Why?" asked Emily with interest.

"Because an old house will nickel-and-dime you to death. That's sage advice from my father, who now lives in a condominium in Florida. But I think we're getting off track here, Emily; I want to talk about your picture. I really like your orange flowers. You're such a good artist."

Sometimes you have to lie so you don't hurt people's feelings, that's what Jon always said. Old ladies and aunts loved him. Whenever he told them they looked pretty, they'd giggle like little girls and then give him money to buy an ice cream or a candy bar. "You don't have to lie to me," Emily told Dr. Radke. "I know I'm a failure as an artist. I even got a B+ in it once."

One of the doctor's thin eyebrows rose up like a question mark. "Do you think if you don't get an A in something it makes you a failure?"

"No," said Emily. "I'm just saying I know I can't draw. My father says writing's a natural talent, something people are born with. I think art's the same way."

Dr. Radke smiled at her. "You're talking to someone who can't draw a stick person, so I'd have to agree with you." Then, turning her attention back to the drawing, she asked, "What's this 'Enter at Your Own Risk' sign mean?"

Emily looked down at the doctor's red fingernail, which was pointing at the sign above the garage. Those were the first words Jon had ever taught her to read. "That's my father's office. He has different signs to let us know if we can bother him while he's writing. Janey says when he's in the Palace the house could burn down and he'd be the last one to know about it."

Dr. Radke laughed. "Palace? Your maid Janey's quite a character."

"Yeah," Emily agreed. "My father's always saying that not even he could make her up."

"You said your father had other signs, too?" Dr. Radke questioned.

Emily nodded. "If 'In the Zone' is on the door it means he's working on something good, so you'd better plan on making your own supper, or if you need a ride to practice you'd better remind him because he won't remember. 'Welcome' means he's just doing revisions, so he can talk to you or sign papers or take phone calls. But 'Enter at Your Own Risk' means what he's working on isn't coming out right, and you'll probably get your head bitten off if you disturb him."

"How clever," said Dr. Radke. "I'd like to have a sign like that myself."

You wouldn't if you had to live with it, thought Emily. The "Enter at Your Own Risk" sign had been hanging on his office door since she'd gotten home from the hospital the first time, way back in April.

"How *is* your father?"

The only time you come out of that damned office is to take a piss or restock your refrigerator with Molson, and don't think I haven't noticed that! That was what her mother had yelled back at her father when he'd said that stuff about her working too much. "Good, I guess," said Emily. "He just about lives in his office these days."

"Is he working on a new book? I really enjoyed his last one."

"He's always working on something."

"Does he ever talk to you about what happened?"

The question felt like a sharp fingernail digging into Emily's skin, and she flinched slightly. The accident was something no one in her family talked about; it just lived in the air around them like all the other unspoken reminders: his smiling pictures, his room, having only three plates at the table. She glared at the crooked picture, suddenly feeling angry. Dr. Radke was always slipping in questions like that to trick her and make her say things about her family she didn't want to. Although this was only her third appointment, she'd already learned that game and how to dodge those kinds of questions. "I'd rather talk about something else," she said politely. *Because that's none of your business.*

Dr. Radke studied her for a moment, as though trying to make a decision. "Like what?" she finally asked.

Like why don't you fix that crooked picture, it's driving me crazy! "Like what I want to be for Halloween."

two

TWENTY MINUTES LATER, Emily rested her head against the back seat of the new Volvo. Exhausted, she let out a sigh and then stared out the window to watch Dr. Radke's brick building disappear for another week. See ya; wouldn't wanna be ya, she thought. Another one of her brother's favorite sayings.

"That sigh was bigger than you are," said Janey from behind the wheel.

Emily caught the maid's concerned glance in the rearview mirror but didn't have the energy to fake a smile.

"If it were up to me, China Doll, that'd be the last time you saw the inside of that place."

Emily closed her eyes and smiled for real. She loved Janey. Just hearing the sound of her voice, even irritated as it now was, made her feel safe. If her brother were here he'd say: Janey's on the warpath; hide while you still can!

"Ask me, some of them mothers in the waitin' room are the ones with the real problems. That one with the bleached do was a beaut, I'll tell ya. I'd be a head case, too, with a mother like that pickin' at me every second. But you listen to Janey, 'cause I know what I'm talkin' about; you ain't like those other kids."

The sharp tone of the maid's voice told her Janey was on her side, but Emily was too preoccupied with thoughts of Jon and of moving to listen. How was she supposed to tell him?

"Only thing eatin' at you is grief, and there's nothing unnatural about that," Janey continued.

When her parents had broken the news of his death to her in the hospital, Emily didn't believe them. Although she couldn't remember much about the accident, she was certain her brother had been with her in the ambulance, could distinctly remember his voice above all that noise, telling her, "Don't worry; I won't leave you." And he hadn't. When she'd gotten home from the hospital sixteen days later, he was waiting for her in the cellar just like he'd promised.

"You got a right to your sorrow, Em," said Janey, turning onto Congress Street. "No matter what your mother says, you wantin' to buy all black back-to-school clothes ain't any red flag to me. Like I told her, 'When I'm feelin' black and blue on the inside I don't feel like wearin' pink.' Jezum-crow, back in the old days that's the way it was when people were in mourning. Widows wore black for a year or more, and for good reason. It told people, 'I lost someone I loved, so don't be messing with me or asking any stupid questions.' Warned them to 'just leave me alone, 'cause I need some time to myself.' But these days it's wham-bam-thank-you-ma'am, don't matter if it's buying a burger or burying the dead. Are you listenin' to me, Em? There's nothing wrong with you that God and time won't heal."

At the sound of her name, Emily opened her eyes and peered out the window just as they passed Longfellow's statue at the corner of State Street. "If we take the new bridge we'll get home a lot faster," she told Janey.

"You might go that way with your mother, but not with me driving," Janey answered. "My cousin Mickey worked on that bridge, and he's not much brighter than a sixty-watt bulb. I'll take the long way before I'll trust a bridge he had anything to do with building. Knowing him, there's bound to be a pile of bolts left over somewhere. Worst thing my mother ever did was letting him build her deck—I say a 'Hail Mary' every time I walk across it so I don't fall through. Judas-priest, even I know you're supposed to use pressure-treated wood so it don't rot out."

Emily took note of that fact and settled back in her seat, knowing it was going to be a long ride—once Janey got started on her relatives, there was no stopping her. Although Janey wasn't married, she had eight brothers and sisters, and so many relatives that they had to rent a hall for their yearly family reunion, an event Janey had taken Emily and her brother to since they were little.

"You know Mickey," Janey continued. "He's always at the reunion. Never known him to miss a free meal. He's the one who shaves his head and can talk like Popeye. But enough about that waste of space—how's your leg doin'?"

Although her leg had been aching all day, that was something she couldn't tell Janey. If she did, Janey wouldn't allow her to practice when she got home, and Emily wouldn't have a reason for going down-cellar. "It feels great," she lied.

The cellar was a huge pine-paneled room with a black-and-white-checked tile floor. It had a pool table and relatively little furniture—a sectional black leather couch, two matching chairs, and a glass-topped wrought-iron coffee table. There were two walls of built-in bookcases, and in the center of another, a fireplace with a black marble hearth and mantel. On one side of the fireplace stood a big-screen TV; on the other, a desk with their computer, and a console for the CD player and stereo system, whose sound came from speakers hidden in the ceiling.

The fourth wall belonged to Emily. Its floor-to-almost-ceiling mirror ran like a silver river along a six-foot section of the wall, and in front of it stood the ballet barre her parents had had built for her when she'd turned seven.

Of the fourteen rooms in their house, this was Emily's favorite. It had been Jon's, too. This was where they'd always hung out together, or with their cousins, or friends from the swim team, or Nate Muldoon from next door. This was where they watched movies, surfed the Net, played board games, shot pool, listened to music. This was where she practiced ballet and he Nintendo, where they'd always held their powwows about their parents, or Janey, or life in general. She figured that was why his spirit lived in the cellar now that he was dead.

It wasn't like she could actually see him, but she could feel him, sometimes so strongly she thought that if she turned quickly enough, or looked up from whatever she was doing, she would see him sitting in one of the black chairs, or leaning over the pool table with a cue stick in his hand.

"Magna trouble," she announced as she crossed the room. "Wait until you hear this!"

She scooped up her ballet shoes off the floor, then flopped into the leather chair and waited for that familiar sensation. But the hairs on the back of her neck didn't tingle, and when she sniffed the air, she didn't smell that fresh scent of his Consort hair gel.

"Wake up!" she demanded. It figured that the one time she had something really important to tell him Jon was taking a nap.

About time, said a familiar voice inside her head.

"It's not my fault," she snapped. "It's Monday, remember? I had to go to that doctor again, and then Janey wouldn't take the new bridge because her cousin Mickey helped build it, so we ended up having to go the long way. Of course that meant stopping by Dairy Queen, because Janey's starting her new diet tomorrow for the millionth time. But none of that's important. What is, is that Mom and Dad had a big fight last night."

She looked down at the pink ballet shoes in her lap. When they were new, the soles had been light gray and the leather rough for traction, but now they were worn to a smooth, shiny black, and the stitching was frayed in places. "At first I thought it was good that they were yelling at each other again—it sounded just like the old days, before they got so quiet and polite you'd hardly know them. But then Mom said she didn't want to come home to this house anymore, and Dad said maybe moving would be the best thing for all of us."

Emily wished she could see the expression on her brother's face. Scared? Mad? Shocked like she'd been, hiding on the stairs, listening in the dark? She glanced over at the picture of him in his baseball uniform. With his sparkling blue eyes and golden-brown hair that was thick and wavy, he looked just like their mother. "Jon looks like me and has my spirit, but Emily's her father's child inside and out"—that was what her mother used to tell people. And they'd always agreed, for Jon had the same straight teeth, quick smile, and big booming laugh that made others laugh when they heard it, and, like her mother, he could never sit still, was always moving. Even when he was sitting, he'd have a leg pumping so fast it could shake the milk in the glasses on the table. His coaches were always saying he was a natural athlete, and that had also come from their mother, who'd been an MVP in three sports in high school, and who, like Jon, hated losing even more than she liked winning.

Move?

"That's what they said, and they must have talked about it before, when I wasn't around." Emily kicked off her sneakers, removed her socks, then slipped her bare feet into her ballet shoes, whose limp elastic straps fell into place on their own.

Why?

"I don't know," said Emily, but then something occurred to her. Without Jon, her mother no longer had a kid who looked just like her or had her spirit. That was probably why she didn't want to come home to their house anymore.

Emily pushed herself out of the chair and headed over to the ballet barre. Without stretching out or warming up, she took hold of the wooden handrail, which was stained in places from so much use, and began doing pliés. "You always were her favorite. And don't say 'No sa,' because you know it's true. If it'd been me that'd broken Gram's 'Little King's' globe, she would have grounded me for a week and made me pay for it out of my allowance, but because it was you, all Mom said was, 'Boys will be boys—don't worry, I'll replace it.'"

His being their mother's favorite had been a frequent argument between them, and her brother's comeback had always been the same—*So what? You're Dad's favorite; you're the one who likes to read and write.*

Hurt and anger sizzled inside her. She moved the arm that wasn't on the barre into second position and did frappés with vigor. "I'm not Dad's favorite, either," she huffed between breaths, "so just keep that thought to yourself. You're the moron who showed him that book report. You just haaad to brag about it. 'Look, Dad, Mrs. Cornelio gave me an A+.' What did you think? He wasn't going to read it?" She swatted at the black strands of hair that had worked their way loose from her braid, then switched sides and began working her good leg. Already the muscles in her left calf were beginning to burn. "It's not my fault Dad knew I wrote it, or that he said those bad things about you. I didn't tell him! If you still don't believe me, now that you're dead you can just ask God."

A second later, her last comment hit her like a slap in the face and she stopped abruptly, one pointed foot still in midair. Although it'd been six and a half months since the accident, she sometimes forgot that her brother was dead—like in the middle of the night, when she woke up from a bad dream and automatically went to his room, or like a moment ago, when she was mad at him.

She let go of the barre and sank to the floor like a deflated balloon. "Sorry," she told him, then ran her hands down her bad leg until they reached the cramp. Wincing, she dug her fingers into the knotted muscle and kept the pressure on, just like her physical therapist had taught her. "See what I get for yelling at you," she said between clenched teeth. She tried to flex her foot gently to relieve the needling pain, and a shivering sensation raced up her leg and settled somewhere in her hip. "I hate you," she told her leg, tears forming in the corners of her eyes. "It's not fair."

And it wasn't. Before the accident she had been the best dancer in her class. Now all the girls were starting pointe except for her. "Maybe next year," her doctor had said as though it didn't matter, as though she hadn't been dreaming about it for years. She'd missed so much: all of last spring, the recital, the solo she'd choreographed herself. She'd had to haul around that external fixitor for four whole months, then a fiberglass cast for four more weeks. She'd thought that when the cast came off everything would be all right, that she'd be the same dancer she was before. But her cast had been off since the middle of August, and despite all the physical therapy, she wasn't the same.

"I can't even do a few pliés without this dumb leg cramping up."

It's your own fault; you should have stretched out first. You know better.

"Shut up," she said because it was true, then glared at her reflection in the mirror, angry with herself for doing something so stupid—and angry at the world.

Maybe you should start swimming again

"You and Dr. Hanley. That's what he told Mom when he took my cast off. Said it would strengthen my muscles without putting any stress on the bones. You should have seen Mom's face—turned whiter than Gram's hair. Thought she was going to faint or something." Imitating her mother's voice, she said, "'I think Emily's more interested in dancing than swimming; she's been taking ballet since she was four.' And then Dr. Hanley must have remembered that you and me and Dad were coming back from a swim meet when it happened, because he told Mom like I wasn't even there, 'I'm sorry, Theresa, I forgot. I completely understand.'" Emily let out a deep sigh. "They don't understand anything."

At least he's letting you dance with Debbie again.

"Yeah, but he made up a zillion rules about it, and pointe's one of them." Every Tuesday and Thursday night, while the other girls in her class worked at the barre in their new pink satin shoes with blocked toes and lovely ribbons crossed and tied perfectly behind their ankles, she had to follow along in the slippers she was wearing now. And as they complained about how hard it was and groaned about the blisters they were getting, she had to keep a smile on her face while she was crying inside.

"You don't know what that feels like. You were always so good at everything, except for maybe school, and even then you got all B's without opening a book or doing any homework.

The only things I was ever good enough at for Mom to brag about were my report card and ballet."

That's not true—you were a good swimmer.

Emily stared past her face in the mirror, her dark-brown eyes searching the reflection of the bookcases behind her. The top shelves were lined with trophies, medals, ribbons, mostly her brother's, but some hers. The day he was killed she'd taken first place in the fifty-meter butterfly, and Jon, as usual, had won all his events. But those medals weren't up there. She wasn't sure what had happened to them and had never had the courage to ask.

"I don't want to start swimming again. It wouldn't be the same being on the team without you." Plus, the only way to get to the pool was down Ruby Road, and she never wanted to see that street again. It was bad enough seeing it in her dreams.

You going to sit there all day and feel sorry for yourself or what?

"You're right," she said, rubbing her leg, her fingers sliding over the raised, tender scar of her skin graft. "I can't waste time on that right now; Mom said she was going to call a Realtor this week, and you know Dad and his signs. I'll probably get home from school tomorrow and there'll be a 'For Sale' one in the front yard. I can't believe him; he told Mom they shouldn't tell me anything until things were definite. When's that supposed to be, when the moving van comes? We've got to think of a way to stop them before that."

She glanced around the cellar, waiting for a sign from her brother, who'd always been the expert on getting out of trouble.

He'd been so good at it that Janey said he could sweet-talk a bum out of his last nickel.

"Come on," pleaded Emily. "You have to think of something. If I tell them we can't move because you're living down here, they'll make me go to Dr. Radke every day for the rest of my life."

The cramp in Emily's leg had finally subsided, but the tight knot of fear in the pit of her stomach was growing. "You know how Mom is when she's got her mind made up about something. It'll be just like that gross flowered wallpaper she picked out for my bedroom last year—what I say or think won't matter. And Dad will go along with her, just like he did then," she said, and, imitating her father, added, "'Don't worry, honey, it will grow on you.'" As if those tacky flowers and ugly colors ever could. Her mother might be the best general surgeon in Portland and great at taking out gallbladders, but when it came to decorating or fashion or shopping, she didn't have a clue. She didn't even know that black was the "in" color this year. Suddenly Emily thought of something.

"Brilliant!" she told her brother, assuming he'd put the great idea into her head. "Who'd want to buy a house like that?"

She'd just started reeling off a list of things she could do when the cellar door opened and Janey's voice bellowed down the stairs.

"Em? Time to call it quits!"

"But why?" Emily yelled back. We just got started!

"'Cause you've been down there practicing enough for one day on that bad leg," said Janey, who, like Emily's parents, never came down-cellar unless she had to. "'Sides, your supper's on the table and it's time for me to leave."

"Okay, okay, I'm coming," Emily called back; then she looked toward the pool table and, with a smile on her face, whispered, "We'll talk about this later."

"And don't forget to shut the lights off this time!" Janey reminded her.

"I won't!" Emily promised.

But after she climbed the stairs and double-checked the cellar door to make sure it was closed tightly, the light beside the computer was still on. No matter what Janey or her father said about how much it cost to pay Central Maine Power, Emily never left her brother down there in the dark.

three

"HURRY UP AND WASH your hands, Em," said Janey. "I've gotta cruise—I'm going to play beano tonight."

"Where's my dad?" Emily asked, noticing that there was only one place set at the kitchen table.

"Said he'd eat later. He's upstairs tryin' to fix that leaky faucet in your parents' bathroom."

Great, thought Emily as she dried her hands. While he had his tools out, maybe she could get him to wreck a few other things.

"And your mother called to say she'd be late. Surprise, surprise."

Emily smiled to herself, thinking, That's probably just what Janey told her, too. Janey was the only person who dared to talk to her mother that way.

The maid banged the refrigerator door shut. "Don't know why I bother to break my back cooking a decent meal that nobody's gonna eat," she said with disgust. Then, a second later, as she poured milk into Emily's glass, she seemed to remember why. "If I left dinner up to your parents, China Doll, you'd be living on hot dogs and takeout and I wouldn't be able to sleep at night. I feel bad enough 'bout you havin' to sit here and eat alone."

Emily glanced over at the empty chair where Jon had always sat. Me, too, she thought. Supper was one of the times she missed him most—cracking her up with his funny stories and jokes, making faces behind Janey's back at the food she'd prepared. If he were there right now and saw those breaded pork chops and gross string beans, he'd grab his throat and make a face like he was being poisoned. And when Janey turned around, like she did just then, he'd tell her the same exact thing Emily now said: "This looks too good to eat."

Janey smiled at her. "I miss hearing him say that," she said, dabbing at her misty eyes. "The little liar always knew the right thing to say."

He still does, thought Emily. She wasn't sure why Janey and her parents didn't know that Jon was living in the cellar, why they couldn't feel or talk to him like she could. She figured part of it was that they rarely went down there, her parents only if they were looking for a book, and Janey maybe once a week to vacuum and dust. There'd been times when she'd been tempted to tell them—like late at night, when she'd hear her mother crying, or that time she'd overheard her dad tell Gram, "It's all my fault," or, like a moment ago, when she'd heard the sadness in Janey's voice. But something always stopped Emily from sharing her secret: the fear that if she told anyone, her brother wouldn't be there waiting for her the next time she walked down those cellar stairs. "It's beano night," she now reminded the maid. "You'd better get going or that Mrs. Winallthetime will get your favorite seat."

"I'm not going anywhere until I get a lucky hug."

Emily jumped up from the table. She closed her eyes as Janey's thick, strong arms wrapped around her, and inhaled the smells of cooking, dish soap, and cigarettes.

"Tighter," Janey told her. "I need all the luck I can get."

When the maid finally let go, the tone of her voice switched to a warning. "And don't you be throwin' your supper in the trash and makin' a peanut-butter-and-jelly as soon as I'm out the door. Ya hear?"

Emily giggled, because that was exactly what she'd planned to do, only she was going to wait until she'd heard Janey's car start up in the driveway, just like Jon had taught her.

"And tell your father I left the plumber's number right by the phone," said Janey as she pulled on her coat. "He'll probably be looking for it in about an hour."

"Okay," Emily told her, but as soon as Janey left, she tore the paper with the number into tiny bits and threw them in the trash.

The first thing Emily saw when she walked into her parents' bathroom was her father's long legs. He was lying on his back, his body hidden from the chest up as he worked beneath the sink's cabinet.

"Hi, Dad," she said, looking down at a pile of her mother's best towels soaking up water on the bathroom floor. "How's it going?"

"Bigger job than I thought it'd be."

Emily grinned; that's what her dad always said when he couldn't fix something. She watched him shimmy out from beneath the cabinet, his face shiny with sweat and his big hands black with grease. Although Emily had her father's brown eyes, straight black hair, and skin that burned even with number-thirty sunscreen, she didn't have his build. He was tall and husky, with a potbelly that rolled over the top of his jeans. She was petite, always the shortest one in her class, and so fine-boned that Janey had been calling her China Doll since she was a baby.

"What time is it?" her father asked, but didn't wait for an answer. "I have to get this finished before your mother gets home."

Emily surveyed the bathroom. Tools were scattered everywhere, and the white-tiled floor, sink, cabinet door, even the toilet-seat cover had smudges of grease on them. Her father was in *big* trouble. "Don't worry," she told him. "Janey talked to her—she's going to be late."

Emily caught the look of relief in her father's eyes and it almost made her feel guilty for tearing up the plumber's number. If her mother walked into this bathroom right now she'd throw a fit.

As though thinking the same thing, her father said, "You've done it now, Ollie."

Emily didn't know who Ollie was, but it was her father's favorite saying when he was in trouble with her mother or did something stupid like taking apart the riding lawn mower, which was still in the shed in a zillion pieces, sitting next to the new one he'd had to go out and buy.

"Janey didn't say how late, did she?" he asked, reaching for a wrench.

"Nope." Just "surprise, surprise." Emily tiptoed carefully across the barrier of towels and took a seat on the tub, which she noticed, just in time, had a black handprint on it, too. "Maybe while you have your tools out, Dad, you can fix the toilet in my bathroom so I don't have to use the one in here."

"One job at a time," answered her father. As he began to disappear back into the cabinet, his broad shoulders barely making it through the small space, his voice turned into a muffled pant. "How'd school go?"

"We met our adopted grandparents at Pleasant Oaks this morning."

"What?"

"It's the community-service project our class is doing this year, remember? We have to go there two mornings a month because some of the old people never get any visitors. You signed the paper."

"If I did, I don't remember."

He didn't even read it, thought Emily—he was probably "In the Zone" and just signed his name. The thing was, now she wished he *hadn't* signed that paper. Pleasant Oaks hadn't been anything like what she'd expected. She'd thought that her adopted grandparent would be someone nice, like her own gram, but Esther wasn't like Gram at all; she had scary blue eyes like a Siberian husky, and hands that were twisted and knobby and gross to look at. And when the nurse introduced them, the first thing Esther had said wasn't "Hello" or "It's nice to meet you" or anything polite like that, it was "You don't look like a boy to me! These people around here can't get anything right."

"Well?" asked her father. "How'd it go?"

"The grandparent I got stuck with is named Esther. She's ninety-four and not very polite."

"When you're ninety-four you don't have to be," said her father. "I think this is a good thing your teacher's doing. And it will give you something to write about."

"Maybe. All I know is I'd never let Gram live in a place like that. It smells just like a hospital, and . . ." Emily didn't finish—the phone was ringing. "I'll get it," she told her father, already limping toward the door that connected the bathroom to her parents' bedroom.

"If it's your mother, I need to talk to her," her father called out from beneath the sink. "If it's my agent, tell him I'm at the medical library doing research."

When she picked up the phone, Emily expected to hear her mother's voice. Instead she heard, "Good evening, this is Loretta Becker from Becker and Brook Realtors. . . ."

Realtors?

". . . May I please speak to your mother?"

A shiver of fear ran through Emily. Her mother hadn't wasted any time. "She's not home right now."

"Oh. Well, may I speak to your father?"

Emily glanced over her shoulder. "He's at the library doing research."

"Would it be possible for you to give your mother a mess
for me, then?"

"Yes."

"Just tell her I returned her call and that Thursday at four is perfect for me."

"Is that all?" Emily questioned.

"That's it. Think you can remember all that, darlin'?"

Duh! "Loretta Becker from Becker and Brook Realtors—Thursday at four is perfect. Correct?"

"Yes, that's right. Thank you."

"You're welcome. Good-bye." Emily punched the off button. In your dreams, lady; my house isn't for sale! Can you remember all that? She threw the phone across her parents' bed.

"Was it Mom?" her father called.

Emily turned her head and glared in his direction. I hate you, she thought. She hated him for telling her mother, "Maybe moving would be the best thing for all of us"; hated him for the scars and the pain, and the loss of her brother. And, deeper still, for that lingering doubt—that he, like her mother, wished it'd been her instead of Jon. "No," she yelled back. "Just one of those stupid telemarketers. I told them my parents are never home."

four

THURSDAY WAS UNCOMMONLY warm for October, a balmy sixty-four degrees by the afternoon, and not a cloud in the blue sky when Emily stepped off the school bus. It was a perfect day for an ambush. If things went as planned, Loretta Becker of Becker and Brook Realtors wouldn't even make it out of her car.

Emily dumped her jacket and backpack on the bench in the kitchen, her eyes already darting toward the cellar to make sure the door was closed. She never entered or left the kitchen without checking. "I'm going out to play," she informed Janey, who was cleaning out the refrigerator on her hands and knees.

Janey's head popped up like a jack-in-the-box. "Now, that's what I like to hear when you come home, Em! 'I'm going out to play,' not, 'I'm going down-cellar to practice.'"

The plan was going more smoothly than Emily had

expected—gauging by the mess in the kitchen, Janey would be tied up for an hour or more.

The maid returned to her scrubbing but kept on talking. "Go on, then; get out there and get some color in those cheeks; you're paler than a ghost these days. And grab one of those apples on your way out. I bought 'em right off the truck at the farmers' market this morning—no bruises on those babies." When Janey looked up a moment later, Emily was gone. Pushing the bangs out of her eyes, the maid mumbled, "Most folks have to beg their kids to practice—that one I have to beg to play. She's either gettin' better or she's up to somethin'."

Fallen leaves crunched under Emily's feet as she cut across the lawn that was now more brown than green. She stopped beneath the maple tree where they'd buried their golden retriever, Sage, and picked up the screwdriver she'd hidden in the dead geraniums. Kneeling down in front of the headstone, whose shellacked wooden surface was starting to weather, she read the epitaph she knew by heart.

Beloved dog and loyal friend.
Remembered in our hearts forever.
Mom, Dad, Jon, and
your special pal, Emily.

She ran her fingertip across the carved letters of Sage's name and for a moment forgot all about the screwdriver, the plan, and the Realtor who was supposed to be arriving in a half-hour.

Sage had been the family's dog, but she'd really belonged to

Emily, who used to call her "Sagey" and "my pal." That's just what they'd been: best pals. Like her brother handing her that flower, her earliest memories of Sage were just as vivid: her face resting against warm fur as they took naps together, the sound of the dog's heartbeat lulling her to sleep. As far back as she could remember, Sagey had always been there to kiss her booboos and eat the food she didn't like. She'd played with her and kept her company when everyone else was too busy, and listened to her troubles when no one else would.

Sage was six years old when Emily was born and lived to be fourteen. When the vet had put Sage to sleep, Emily had cried all day, and for many nights afterward. They'd buried Sagey beneath the maple tree, where she'd liked to sleep on hot days, where she and Emily used to snuggle together in the shade while Emily read for hours. The casket was a cardboard box lined with her favorite blanket and, tucked beneath her paw, Emily had placed her pal's favorite ball. During the funeral, everyone in her family had said something nice about Sage, but when it was her turn, Emily was crying too hard to talk. If she could have, she would have told them about the time the two of them had eaten that icicle together after rolling in the snow, or how Sagey was always waiting for her at the end of the driveway when the school bus brought her home. But the only words stuck in Emily's throat were the ones she'd screamed out her bedroom window as she'd watched her father's truck leave for the vet's; her pal lying on the front seat, going for her last ride: "Oh, Sagey! My Sagey!"

Emily's thoughts turned from Sage to her brother. She'd been in the hospital when they'd buried him on the twenty-first of March. Unlike with Sagey, she'd never gotten to see or touch him one last time. She didn't know what his casket looked like or what he'd been wearing—didn't get to place something favorite inside for him to have with him, didn't get to cut a few locks of his hair and save them in a tiny bag in the bottom of her ballerina jewelry box like she had with her dog. They'd taken that chance away from her, had made her stay in the hospital while everyone else got to say good-bye. Now, as she picked up the screwdriver by its silver shaft, she silently vowed, No one will ever take anything away from me again.

At the end of their long, tree-lined driveway there was a black lantern post that sported their street number in brass. Once the brass numbers had been removed, Emily threw them away in the culvert along with the screws that had held them to the post. The third thing on her "to do" list had been taken care of.

With a sense of accomplishment, she started limping back up the winding driveway, stopping for just a moment, when her house came into view. The three-story colonial looked beautiful in the golden autumn light. When she was little, it used to be white with black shutters, but her parents had it repainted the summer her father's eighth novel, a medical mystery, made the best-seller list. By the time *People* magazine and all the others came to interview him, her house had been changed to pale yellow with white trim, the black shutters replaced by ones of dark forest green.

Stationing herself on the front step of the breezeway, Emily watched the driveway and waited for the enemy. She was a listener and always remembered what people said, especially her father: "Be creative, but write about what you know. . . . A misspelled word in a final draft is unacceptable. . . . Pay attention to detail and do your research." She'd done her research. It hadn't taken her any time at all to find the Becker and Brook Realtors Web site on the Internet. She knew all about the woman whose black Porsche was, at that moment, coming up the Racines' driveway.

Emily was at the driver's-side window before the woman even had a chance to shut the car off. "Are you Loretta Becker?" she asked sweetly.

"Oh," said the startled woman, whom Emily had just caught checking out her lipstick in the visor's mirror. "I didn't . . . Yes, I'm Loretta."

"Don't bother to shut your car off," Emily told her. "My mother just got called in for an emergency case. She said to tell you she was very sorry. She's going to have her secretary call your office to set up a new time."

"Oh," the woman repeated, but this time with disappointment. She glanced at the gold watch on her wrist. "I don't have another appointment until six; I could wait for her if . . ."

"It's a bowel obstruction," Emily interrupted. "She won't be home until really late."

To her surprise, Loretta shut the car off. "Well, since I'm already here, I don't think she'll mind if I take a little look-see."

Emily felt a stab of panic and glanced over her shoulder at the house, where Janey was, she hoped, still cleaning in the kitchen and her father still writing in the Palace. "She probably wouldn't mind," she said, "but my father would. He's a famous writer and he doesn't like people to interrupt him when he's working. That's how the first lady got fired."

"First lady?" inquired Loretta.

"From Century 21," said Emily, remembering Loretta had once worked for them, had, in fact, been their top seller for three consecutive years before starting her own business in 1992. "You probably know her, their signs are everywhere. I think she's even in a commercial."

"Margaret Cummings?"

Emily, who was making things up as she went, said, "That might be the one. She had blond hair and was really pretty."

"I wouldn't go that far," remarked Loretta, "but the last time I saw her, she did have what could pass for blond hair. Your mother must have forgotten to mention to me that your house had already been listed by Margaret."

"I'm not sure what 'listed' means, but she never got past our living room." Emily shook her head as though the memory were a bad one. "You know what writers are like when they have a deadline. They have wicked bad tempers. I tried to tell that lady he wouldn't want to be interrupted, but she wouldn't listen to me. My mother was probably too embarrassed to tell you about it."

"I see."

It's working, thought Emily. Through the windshield of her car, Loretta Becker was staring at their house like a crazy man was going to come running out the front door any second.

The woman turned and gave Emily what her father would have called a plastic smile. "Maybe I should come back another time, when your mother can be here."

"You're a lot smarter than that other lady," said Emily with feigned sincerity.

The real-estate agent's smile grew wider. "Yes, Margaret can be rather pushy."

"My parents like intelligent people who listen to directions."

"So do I," said the woman, and then, to Emily's relief, she started up her car. "Thank you for your help, darlin'."

"You're welcome. I just hope I don't get in trouble for telling you about that Margaret lady."

Loretta pressed a finger against her bright-red lips. "That will be our little secret."

"I think that's a smart decision," Emily told her. "Bye, now." She walked over to the lawn so she was out of the way and, from there, watched the car turn around and head back down the driveway. *She looks a lot older than the picture on her homepage,* thought Emily, *but Jon would love her car—it looks just like the Batmobile.*

Although Emily had gotten rid of Loretta Becker of Becker and Brook Realtors in less than four minutes, it was just in time.

"Who was that?" asked Janey, opening the door.

Emily turned and looked at her, then shrugged. "Just some lady who was lost. She thought this was the Daleys' house. But don't worry, I gave her the right directions."

"Next time, you come and get me," Janey told her. "I don't want you talking to strangers. Little girl got kidnapped right out of her own front yard last year down in Florida. You can't trust anyone these days."

"I know," said Emily. *Sometimes not even your parents.*

five

THE PLAN TO AMBUSH the real-estate agent went perfectly, but as Emily told her brother, "That won't be the last we hear from her."

And she was right. The following week, when her mother said casually, "I thought maybe you'd like to have an overnight at Gram's this weekend," Emily knew for certain that Loretta Becker had gotten tired of waiting for the phone call that Emily's mother's secretary was never going to make.

"It has to be that," Emily told her brother as she warmed up in front of the ballet barre. "Why else would Mom want to get rid of me this weekend? I bet you a zillion dollars that Becker the Home Wrecker is coming to look at the house. She must have finally gotten Mom at the office, because I erased the message she left on our answering machine."

Emily lifted the heel of her foot onto the barre and slowly began to stretch out. Even though she'd known the real-estate agent would eventually get in touch with her mother again, she hadn't expected it to be that fast. "We should have sent that fax, like I told you. She probably wouldn't have called back so soon if she thought Mom was away on vacation in Europe. That's the last time I let you talk me out of a good idea."

She touched the toes of her foot with her fingertips and, resting her head on her arm, stared at herself in the mirror. "What now, brown cow? It's too early for plan B yet. All I know is I don't want that witch in our house without me around. But the only way they wouldn't ship me off to Gram's on Saturday was if . . . Yeah, that would work. I'm feeling sick already."

As it turned out, Emily didn't have to use the oatmeal-in-the-toilet trick her brother had taught her to pretend she was sick. On Friday morning when she woke up, she vomited for real.

"Don't cry, honey, it's okay," her mother told her as she washed up Emily in the bathroom for the second time in ten minutes. "Just try to relax and take a couple of slow, deep breaths for me."

The washcloth felt good on the back of Emily's neck, but her stomach was still grinding and tight with cramps. "I'm never eating Mexican food again," she moaned.

Her mother placed the back of her hand on Emily's clammy forehead. "I doubt it's that; you're running a fever. You most likely have that virus that's been going around."

While her mother was helping her get into clean pajamas, Emily felt like she was on the merry-mixer at the fair and had to lean on her mother just to keep herself from toppling over. The whirling inside her head eased up a little once she was lying down in her parents' bed.

"Dad will be in just as soon as he's finished cleaning up your room," her mother said, tucking the down comforter around Emily's shoulders. "And I've put the wastebasket right here by the bed in case you can't make it to the bathroom in time."

But I don't want to puke again, thought Emily, and, looking up at her mother, she pleaded, "Can't you stay home with me?"

"You know I would if I could, Em."

"Just this one time, Mom? Please?"

"I can't, honey. I have three cases this morning, and if I don't make my seven-thirty start time the OR will probably bump my first patient. You know I can't let that happen."

Emily turned her head away. When I grow up and have kids I'm going to stay home with them and just be a mother, she thought. She turned over on her side and curled up in a ball. She was feeling sick again and closed her eyes to stop the bed from spinning.

"That's it, Em," her mother said softly, as she gently rubbed circles on her back. "Sleep's the best medicine for this flu."

"How's the patient?" Emily heard her father ask somewhere above her, but her head was throbbing so badly she didn't want to open her eyes or even move her lips to answer, I'm dying.

"A hundred and two," her mother told him. "Don't give her anything to eat. Just some Tylenol and a little flat ginger ale if she can keep it down. I'll call between cases to check on her."

"You don't look too good yourself," her father said.

"I don't have time to be sick," her mother told him. "I'm running late enough as it is."

Emily felt her mother's cool lips on her cheek and a final pat on her back, and her last thought before drifting off into a restless sleep was, She doesn't have time for me, either.

In her dream, Emily was lying on a table staring up at lights that looked like flying saucers. She kept asking, "Where's my brother?" but the blue smurfs who had eyes but no mouths wouldn't tell her. "We have to take good care of her," she heard someone whisper. "She's Dr. Racine's daughter." She wanted to run away, but they'd strapped her to the table with a seatbelt, and she couldn't get loose. Then one of the smurfs took her arm and put it on a board. "You might feel a little bee sting," he said, and that's when she saw the needle in his hand. She struggled to free her arm from his rubbery grip, tried to fight, but there were too many of them, and they were leaning on her and holding her down. "I want my brother!" she screamed, and woke up with a shiver and an awful taste in her mouth.

The dream's icy fingers still had a hold on her, and that overwhelming instinct to run caused her head to jerk right off the pillow. Heart still racing, she glanced around her parents' bedroom, whose windows let in streams of late-morning sun. Just seeing the pale-blue walls and familiar furniture made her breathe easier. I'm safe, she told herself. Just another bad dream.

She pulled up the comforter that she'd kicked off in her sleep and stared at the patch of blue sky through the window, trying to get warm again. Far off she heard the sound of footsteps running up the stairs, which grew louder as they came down the hall. Suddenly her father was standing in the doorway, panting.

"You okay?" he asked. "Are you going to be sick again?"

Emily poked her chin over the comforter and in a hoarse whisper answered, "I hope not."

"Oh," he said with relief. "I thought I heard you yelling for help." Her father sat down on the edge of the bed and, leaning over her, placed a hand on her forehead. "You're hot as a cannon. We need to get some Tylenol into you. How's your stomach feeling?"

"Thirsty," she said. "My throat feels like it's on fire."

Her father smiled at her. "Good description." From a tray on the nightstand he picked up a glass of ginger ale. "I brought this up earlier but you were sleeping. Here, take just a couple of sips."

Emily's hands were shaky as she held the glass to her dry lips. The ginger ale felt good in her mouth, but her throat was so sore it was hard to swallow.

Reading the thermometer a few minutes later, her father said, "A hundred and three. Some kids will do anything to take a day off from school."

"Don't," Emily told him. "It kills to laugh."

After giving her Tylenol and a fresh washcloth for her forehead, her father surprised her with a book she hadn't seen in years—a condensed version of Longfellow's *Hiawatha,* with great illustrations by Susan Jeffers.

"I found it while I was cleaning my office," he said, stretching out on the bed beside her. "You used to make me read it to you every night when you were little. Remember?"

Emily's glassy eyes gazed at the picture of Hiawatha on the cover. "I remember," she whispered. When she was in kindergarten, her teacher, Mrs. Tibbits, had told her she'd make a good Native American in their Thanksgiving play because she had long black braids. But it was the book in her father's hands that had made Emily want to be one. To her, she wasn't Girl Number Two in the play; she was Nokomis, the loving, wise Daughter of the Moon. She'd had her three lines memorized by the end of their first rehearsal, and by the end of the first week, everyone else's as well. She went around the house pretending she was Nokomis, and practicing, "We have brought corn to share with you," over and over in all different ways. For two weeks her class made decorations for their room and costumes and props for the skit they would perform in front of their parents. Emily couldn't wait for her mother to see her in the headdress she'd so carefully made out of construction paper, feathers, and glitter-glue, couldn't wait for her to watch her say the lines in the same graceful way Nokomis would. Her mother had promised that she'd be there, but only her father and Janey had come. It was then that Emily realized her mother's patients would always come first.

"You used to walk around the house with a pigeon feather in your hair and tell everyone your name wasn't Emily, it was Nokomis." Her father chuckled. "You were so cute."

"What else did I do?" asked Emily, wondering if he remembered that Thanksgiving play and how, as soon as it was over, she'd torn up the headdress because her mother hadn't come.

"I remember, when I took you and Jon to Longfellow's house, you told the tour guide who was taking us through, 'My father's a writer, but he's not as good as Longfellow.'"

"I did not," she croaked, pushing a small fist into her father's side.

"You did." He laughed. "But don't worry, you were just telling the truth. Now, snuggle up and save your voice; I'll do the reading."

Emily rested her head against her father's shoulder and stared at the intricate illustration of the forest and wigwams, geese in flight, and Nokomis cradling Hiawatha as his mother's spirit watched from above.

"By the shores of Gitche Gumee," her father began in his deep, rich reading voice.

Closing her tired eyes, Emily listened to the story she'd known so well when she was little and life was safe. The rhythm of its words and the sound of her father's voice soothed the aching in her head and seemed to numb the ever-present pain that lived inside her.

"Heard the whispering of the pine-trees,
Heard the lapping of the water,
Sounds of music, words of wonder . . ."

Lulling her to sleep like the comforting murmur of Sagey's heartbeat.

The sound that jarred Emily from her dreamless sleep an hour later wasn't as pleasant. Her mother always kept the switch on the bedside phone on loud so its ring would be sure to wake her in the middle of the night when she was on call. The ear-piercing *brrring* echoed in Emily's skull like a fire alarm and sent her fumbling for the phone. She managed to pick it up just as her father said "Hello" on the other end. Still groggy and confused, Emily stared over at the empty spot where he had been reading to her what seemed like only a second ago.

"Is this Mr. Racine?"

Emily recognized the voice at once; suddenly she was completely awake, the sleepy cobwebs swept from her brain. She quickly covered the receiver with her palm so they wouldn't hear her breathing.

"Yes, it is," her father answered.

"This is Loretta Becker, the real-estate agent who's been working with your wife. I hate to disturb you at home, Mr Racine—I know you're a writer and how frustrating it must be to have someone interrupt you while you're working—but I'm afraid I didn't have a choice, as I've been unable to reach Dr. Racine."

"Thank you for being so considerate, Ms. Becker, but let me assure you, I'd rather have you call here than disturb my wife when she's in the OR."

"I'm relieved to hear you say that, because that's exactly how I felt, too, when her office told me she was in surgery. And trust me, I wouldn't have bothered you, either, if this wasn't so important. But you see, I have a couple who are very interested in seeing your house just from the lovely description your wife gave to me over the phone. The husband is being transferred to the Portland area. The computer company he works for just bought the Chase building downtown; you might have read about it in the paper.

"Anyway, he and his wife, who is a buyer for Borders, are looking in your price range, and I didn't want to let the opportunity to show your house slip by us while they're up here from New York looking for houses this weekend. I thought that, since I was already coming tomorrow, I could kill two birds with one stone and . . ."

"But you haven't even seen our house yet," Emily's father interrupted. "How do you know what it's worth?"

Uh-oh, thought Emily as she listened to Loretta pause on the other end. What if she tells him she's been here?

"I know what houses in your neighborhood go for, Mr. Racine. I just sold one on Ocean View Drive."

Phew, thought Emily.

"I see," said her father.

"It's a sellers' market right now, Mr. Racine, and if you're really serious about selling yours, now is the time. Please don't misunderstand me. I'm not in the habit of pressuring clients, that's not my style; I wouldn't be as successful as I am if it were. But the Johnsons are very anxious, and I'm scheduled to show them several other properties tomorrow; I just didn't want you to miss this chance. However, if you want to discuss it with your wife first, I can give you my pager number so you can reach me."

Now it was her father's turn to pause.

Tell her she can't come, Dad, Emily silently willed. Tell her your daughter's too sick. Tell her I puked all over my bed this morning. Tell her I have that virus that's going around and she might catch it and die and never be able to sell another house again.

"Well, we were planning on meeting with you anyway, so I don't think Theresa would have a problem with that."

"Excellent," replied Loretta. "I'll plan on getting there a little earlier—say, ten-thirty? That way I'll be able to have a walk-through before I show it to them at eleven. Now that that's settled, I won't take up any more of your valuable time. Unless, of course, you have any questions."

"I can't think of any, except, well, do they have any children?"

"Yes, they do. Three girls—all teenagers. I can't imagine what that must be like," Loretta said with a tittering laugh that to Emily sounded just like a chattering squirrel. "But having three bathrooms and being in an excellent school system will definitely be strong selling points."

"I suppose they will," said her father. "We'll see you tomorrow, then."

"I'm looking forward to it," answered Loretta. "Good-bye."

And good riddance, thought Emily. She waited for them to hang up, then replaced the phone on the hook. I have to sneak down-cellar and talk to Jon. It's plan B for sure now.

By the time she reached the back stairs Emily was feeling dizzy. Taking hold of the railing, she told herself the same thing her mother had said that morning: "I don't have time to be sick."

She hadn't even tiptoed down two steps when Janey's voice echoed up the stairwell from the kitchen below.

"I can understand her wantin' a change. I can't go in his

room without it breakin' my heart—no more dirty laundry to pick up off the floor, no empty ice-cream bowls."

"It's not just her, Janey. It's me. I need to get out of here, too. I haven't been able to write a decent page of this book since it happened. I just sit up there looking out the window, thinking about him."

"Changing houses isn't going to solve your problem, Michael. And don't think I don't know about it. Remember, I'm the one who takes the bottles back. Ask me, if you did more thinkin' instead of drinkin' you'd be writin' again, so don't be usin' that sweet boy's death as any excuse around me."

"I was driving, Janey."

"Yes, you were, but it could've been me, could've been Theresa. Wouldn't have made a difference who was drivin'—black ice is black ice. Ain't no one who lives in Maine don't know that when you hit it all you can do is go for the ride. So stop blamin' yourself for somethin' you couldn't stop or help, or you're gonna lose more than you already have, 'cause this family's fallin' apart. Theresa eatin' like a bird and lookin' like a skeleton and workin' herself to death like a dog. Em livin' down in that cellar or in a book and eatin' supper by herself all the time. You hidin' in the Palace, tryin' to drink away your guilt. It kills me to tell you, but it's killin' me worse to watch."

"Why do I suddenly feel like I'm sitting in my mother's kitchen?"

"Because your mother's a smart woman," said Janey. "And if she was here right now she'd tell you it's about time you gave me another raise."

"You deserve one. And you're right . . . about everything."

"Don't be pattin' me on the back yet, 'cause I ain't finished. You can't have those people strollin' through this house tomorrow without tellin' Em what's goin' on."

"This is turning into a mess, Janey. We had planned to have her stay at my mother's, and after we showed the real-estate agent the house, Theresa and I were going to go out looking at houses on our own. But now, with Emily sick, and that couple coming, I guess I'm going to have to tell her."

I'd better go down the front stairs, thought Emily, or they'll know I've been listening. A minute later she limped through the kitchen's main doorway, just as Janey said, "That little girl's been through a lot of changes. Just don't expect her to be happy about it."

"Happy about what?" asked Emily, as if she didn't have a clue what they were talking about. She saw Janey and her father exchange glances; then she rubbed her eyes and gave a pretend yawn, as though she'd just awakened.

"What are you doin' down here?" scolded Janey. "You should be upstairs in bed."

Emily gave Janey her best "I'm sick" look and then a cough for good measure. "I just wanted some ginger ale. It hurt my throat too much to yell for you."

"All glassy-eyed and no slippers on your feet." Janey put her arms around Emily and gave her a kiss on the forehead. "At least you don't feel as warm as you did when I checked on you before. Are you hungry yet, China Doll?"

Emily rested her head against Janey and nodded.

"That's a good sign, but we'd better start you off slow. I'll get you some ginger ale and make you a little dry toast." Janey let go of her. "Now, you go over and sit with your daddy, 'cause he's got somethin' he needs to tell you. Right, Michael?"

Looking worried, her father nodded. "Come here, Em," he said in a serious voice. He took his jacket off the chair and draped it over her shoulders, then lifted her up into his lap. She settled against him, and remembered how he'd read *Hiawatha*, how he'd come running into the room all out of breath just because he'd thought she'd called for him. For a second, when she looked up into his sad brown eyes, she wanted to tell him: Don't worry, I already know.

"This might be hard for you to understand, Em, but, well, your mother and I are thinking of moving."

"Where?"

"We don't know yet, but don't worry, honey, it wouldn't be far. You'd still be going to the same school and everything, and Janey would still be with us. It's just, after all we've been through, your mother and I thought it'd be easier living in a different house and a different neighborhood, so . . ."

You can forget him?

". . . you'd have kids your own age to play with . . . where we wouldn't be reminded every day and all the time that your brother's no longer here."

But he *is* here, she thought, looking over at the closed cellar door. And I won't let you take him away from me again!

"So that's why some people are coming to look at our house tomorrow—to see if they'd like to buy it."

"Is that all?" Emily asked as though it were no big deal, as if her father had just told her the weather or the time. "Boy, from the way you said it might be hard for me to understand, I thought you were going to tell me you had cancer or that Mom and you were getting a divorce or something awful like that."

Emily climbed out of her father's lap and went over to where the maid was fixing her toast. "Can I take my toast and drink upstairs, Janey? I'm getting cold again."

"Of course you can. Now, go hop into bed; I'll bring it up to you. And if you don't have any trouble keepin' toast down, Janey will make you a nice bowl of chicken-noodle soup and some of your favorite red Jell-O. Don't worry, China Doll, I'll have you back on your feet in no time."

I hope so, thought Emily. *Jon and I have a lot of work to do tonight.* "Thanks, Janey."

"You're welcome, baby. And this time take the back stairs so you don't have so far to walk."

Although Emily did what she was told, she waited long enough on the stairs to hear her father say, "That went better than I ever expected," and for Janey to answer, "Kids—go figure."

six

EMILY HAD SLEPT so much on Friday, she was wide awake and ready to go to work at three in the morning on Saturday. Using the flashlight she kept under her pillow so she could read at night when she wasn't supposed to, she crept along the upstairs hall; down the back stairs; through the kitchen, where she grabbed a handful of cookies; and down to the cellar.

"Rise and shine," she told her brother. "Time to go to plan B."

The room was so cold that, by the time Emily set her cookies on the coffee table and grabbed the afghan off the couch, her teeth were clicking. "Feels like a refrigerator in here," she said, watching her breath float out in front of her like a cloud. Having wrapped the afghan around her, she sat down on the couch and for a moment just stared at the small lamp she always left on for him, fascinated with the shadows cast by its dim light. To her it looked just like Jon with his baseball cap on, and suddenly the room didn't feel as cold.

For the next few minutes she talked to the shadow, filling Jon in on the phone call between her father and Loretta Becker and the conversation she'd overheard between her father and Janey.

"Never let a reader know where a story's going—how many times have you heard Dad say that one?" questioned Emily.

A zillion.

"Yeah, at least. So I just followed his advice. I let him and Janey think I was so happy he didn't have cancer and wasn't getting divorced from Mom that I didn't care about moving at all. See, that way they won't suspect me when no one wants to buy our house."

Good thinking, Einstein.

"Thanks."

And Mom?

"She wants to move so bad it was even easier convincing her. I think I'm getting to be as good a liar as you. Okay, well, maybe not as good, but it was just like you telling the old ladies they looked pretty—Mom was wanting to give me all kinds of things. You should have heard her. She said she was going to look for a house in a neighborhood where there were kids my age and where I could ride my bike and be close enough to school so I could walk. And then she promised me she'd buy all new furniture for my room and that this time she'd even let me pick out my own wallpaper. If I hadn't already puked that morning, I would have right then. It really made me sick—as if I'd ever give you up for some lousy furniture or a place where I could ride my bike. Made me wonder what she'd offer you if I was the one living down here—a neighborhood with a skateboard park?"

Emily bit into her third cookie and chewed thoughtfully. "You're right, we can't sit around feeling sorry for ourselves; I have too much work to do. That witch Loretta will be here at ten-thirty, and you know Mom, she's always up at the crack of dawn even on her day off, so I have to get moving." Emily got off the couch and with a sense of purpose headed for the stairs. Before starting up the steps, she looked over once again at the shadow that she was certain was her brother's and told him one last thing. "I don't care what Dad says; I'll remember you every day and all the time. And don't worry, when I'm done with these people, they'll never want to see our house again, never mind buy it." With that she went up the stairs and closed the cellar door tightly behind her.

Much to Emily's surprise, her mother didn't get up at the crack of dawn as usual. In fact, Emily got so tired of waiting for the sound of her footsteps in the hall that, by the time the windows in her bedroom began to grow light, she couldn't keep her eyes open any longer. Two and a half hours later, the first question she asked her father as she plodded into the kitchen was the same one she'd asked herself before she'd fallen back to sleep. "Where's Mom?"

Her father, who was pouring a glass of ginger ale, looked over at her. "I'm afraid she has the same flu bug as you," he said. "She's so sick she can't even get out of bed. I told her we should just cancel this thing today, but she won't let me. How are you feeling?"

Emily's slippers made a sticking sound as she crossed the floor she'd mopped with apple juice at about four o'clock that morning. "Tired," she told him truthfully, but she could tell her father wasn't even listening. He had that "In the Zone" look in his eyes. Just to test him, she said, "I got an F on my book report."

"That's good," he answered automatically, then tried to put the ginger-ale bottle in the cabinet instead of the refrigerator.

He's really out of it, thought Emily. This would be a good time to ask him for some money to buy that Goo Goo Dolls CD.

The bottle of soda was too tall to fit on the shelf. "What am I doing?" her father scolded himself. "This house stuff is already driving me crazy. Your mother's sick one day out of the year and it has to be today. Think you can make your own breakfast, Em?"

Her first thought was, Don't I always? Her second: Pancakes would make a good mess. "Sure. You just take care of Mom."

With an edge of desperation in his voice, her father considered another possibility. "Maybe I should give Janey a call and see if she could come over this morning."

Uh-oh, thought Emily. Her parents might not notice that she'd washed the living-room windows with Lemon Pledge, but Janey would. Panic was just starting to grip her when she remembered, "Saturday's the day Janey takes the retired nuns grocery shopping at Shaw's."

"Retired what?" her father asked.

"The old nuns that live on the same street as Janey, in that house beside the church with the scary-looking Jesus on it. You know, the ones she's always telling us funny stories about—Sister Bernie, and Sister St. Clair, and the one she just calls Mother."

"Right, right, right—how could I forget that great line?"

"Which one?" asked Emily. Janey had so many good ones when she got going on her nun stories.

"The one when she told the head nun, 'Mother, I'm a sinner and you're not, you don't save me, I won't corrupt you, and we'll get along fine.'"

"That's not how it went, Dad. It's 'You don't try to change me and I won't try to change you, and everything will be hunky-dory.'"

"Hmm, maybe you're right. 'Hunky-dory' does sound like Janey."

"And 'corrupt' sounds like you."

"That's a perfect example, Em, of why I tell you to write things down when you hear them so you won't forget."

Her father was always writing down lines like Janey's, or bits of dialogue, or sayings, even names of streets and people he came across that he liked. He'd jot them down on anything: napkins in restaurants, paper bags, candy-bar wrappers found beneath the seat of the car. Then he'd record them in a huge orange notebook in his office along with the date, and sooner or later that line or name or whatever it happened to be would show up in one of his short stories or books. But, unlike her father, Emily never went to that trouble; she just remembered those things in her head. "I like your version better, but I'll bet you five dollars I'm right. Check your orange book and see."

Her father glanced up at the kitchen clock. "I'm afraid I don't have time to do that right now, honey. That real-estate agent will be here before I know it, and I have to get this up to your mother and pick up the house and . . ."

"Don't worry, Dad," Emily interrupted, "I'll help you. Just make sure Mom stays in bed." So I can mess things up a little more.

"Your mother's always saying doctors and nurses are the worst patients for a reason, Em. She's not going to listen to me."

"Well, if I was those people, I'd rather miss seeing Mom's room than watching her puke."

"Good point," her father agreed. "That might keep her in bed."

She hadn't been able to tell from Loretta Becker's pictures on the Internet or from seeing her sitting in her Porsche how tall she was, so when Emily answered the door and found herself eye-level with the woman's briefcase, it took her by surprise. Tilting her head backward, she stared up at her and Jon's enemy, her confidence momentarily evaporating until she spotted the woman's earrings. Definite fashion crime.

"Good morning," said the woman in a chirpy voice, her eyes already looking past Emily for a glimpse of the main hallway.

They look like dinner plates hanging off her lobes, thought Emily.

"Lovely entry," Loretta mused and barged right by Emily for a better look.

She could probably knock somebody out with one of those earrings if she turned her head too quick, Emily figured.

"Real marble floor, and a staircase to die for—I can just picture white lights and greenery decorating that beautiful mahogany railing at Christmas," said Loretta as though she were trying to sell some invisible client the handrail that Emily had carefully polished with grape jelly in the wee hours of the morning. "The table's a nice touch, too, but the vaahz definitely has to go."

Emily scooted around the woman's long legs and stood protectively in front of the hall table. "My gram gave us that vase and it's not going anywhere."

Loretta looked down at her as though she'd just remembered who'd let her in. "I'm sorry, darlin', why, you're so quiet and pretty and polite, I forgot you were even here. I apologize; sometimes I forget my manners when I'm working inside my head. Why don't you run along now like a good little girl and let your mother know that Loretta Becker has arrived just a hair early."

Emily could feel the anger heating up her cheeks. She wanted to say something mean, something really impolite, like, Those are the ugliest earrings I've ever seen—but of course she didn't. "My mother's sick, but if you wait right here, Ms. Becker, I'll let my father know you've arrived twenty-four minutes early."

"That's okay, Em, I'm right here," said her dad from the top of the stairs.

Emily watched him lumber down the steps, relieved that he hadn't bothered to use the handrail.

"Michael Racine," he said, reaching out his hand. "Nice to meet you."

Don't get too close, Dad! If one of those earrings falls off, it'll break your foot!

The real-estate agent shook his hand as though he were the Pope or the President. "Loretta Becker," she said. "And it's a pleasure to meet you in person. I must confess, I'm a big fan of yours. *Final Decisions* was such an excellent book, I couldn't put it down until I finished it."

Oh, great, thought Emily, they're probably going to be best friends now—her father liked anyone who read his books.

"Thank you," he said. "That's always nice to hear."

"I sincerely enjoy a mystery that's not only realistic but has a powerful message behind it. Why, with HMOs all over the news these days, I'm sure it's only a matter of time before Hollywood makes that book into a movie."

Don't listen to her, Dad; she's just trying to shmooze you. "Sincerely enjoy"—how lame can you get!

"In fact, I enjoyed it so much that I bought four copies to give as gifts, and I thought that maybe, if it wasn't too much of an imposition, you might sign them for me?"

Oh God, thought Emily, this woman *is* good.

"Of course I would," said her father, who, to Emily's dismay, was puffing up like a proud rooster.

Emily needed to bring her dad back to earth. "Hardcover or paperback?" she asked Loretta.

That question got her father's attention quick enough. He shot her a parent look that said, "That's rude," but Emily was more interested in Loretta's reaction. The woman's plastic smile slipped just long enough to let them know the answer.

Paperback, thought Emily; point for me. Then she tried for another: "Sorry, Ms. Becker, even though my father makes more money on hardcovers, I'm not supposed to ask that. Sometimes I forget my manners when I'm working inside my head. It's sort of like you telling me that the vase my gram brought back from Virginia has to go."

Despite all her makeup, the woman's face suddenly seemed whiter.

"Kids," said her father, as though it were enough of an apology.

Loretta quickly recovered and nodded with enthusiasm. "I hear you. My youngest sister has four boys under the age of ten. You can imagine what that's like!"

Emily caught the sad smile on her father's face and knew he was trying to imagine what it'd be like having four boys like the son he'd just lost. "She must have her hands full," he said quietly.

"Yes," Loretta answered with a coy smile. "And, thankfully, she still lives down in North Carolina with that little herd of ankle-biters."

Emily expected her father to laugh, but he didn't. "Why don't I show you around, Ms. Becker," he said abruptly, as if he were bored or irritated or had just seen through that plastic smile for the first time.

Must have finally noticed those earrings, thought Emily. Time to go; she didn't want to be around when her father saw the mess she'd made in the kitchen. Still, she warned him. "I made you blueberry pancakes for breakfast, Dad. I'm going upstairs now to clean my room." I need to take down the rest of my posters so those people can get a good look at that gross wallpaper.

"Cooks and cleans," Loretta exclaimed. "Does she do windows, too?"

Yeah, thought Emily, as she made a hasty retreat up the stairs. Check out the ones in the living room.

Now that the leaves were mostly gone from the trees, Emily could see the Muldoons' house from where she sat on the front porch. For the past half an hour she'd been watching two of the Muldoon brothers, Nate and Eric, rake leaves. Nate was fourteen and had been friends with her brother since they were old enough to build snow forts and make burglar traps. Before Jon died, Nate had just about lived at their house. Now he never came over anymore, though he sometimes waved at her from a distance.

If she had her father's binoculars with her, she'd watch Nate and Eric up close, like she did from her bedroom window. Spying on the Muldoons was always an option when she had nothing else to do, because with three teenage boys, there was always something good going on. Joe, the oldest, who was a senior in high school and a basketball star, usually had half the team over there, and sometimes they'd get to playing so hard during a game that someone would get hurt or a fight would break out, and that was always fun to watch. So was watching Eric and his high-school friends, whom Janey called "wannabe hippies." But mostly she liked spying on Nate. He was cute, and she missed not having him hanging around.

For the umpteenth time, she checked her watch. The people from New York were already twenty minutes late. If they didn't come soon, her father and Becker would have the kitchen all cleaned up. Before she'd escaped out the front door, she'd heard them in there laughing and took a peek. Her father was busy packing the dishwasher, and Ms. Becker had her suit coat off and her sleeves rolled up, and was scrubbing away at the blueberry mess on the counter.

New activity over at the Muldoons' recaptured her attention. Mr. Muldoon, a lawyer who made so much money his wife could just lie around by their pool all day, was coming out of the house carrying a present. He was followed a minute later by his wife, and again Emily found herself wishing she had the binoculars to get a better look at Mrs. Muldoon's outfit. Although her mother liked to say that Mrs. Muldoon was going to look like a raisin and have skin cancer by the time she was fifty, Emily thought she was cool. The only reason she liked to go to church on Sunday was to see what Mrs. Muldoon was wearing. Nate's mother really knew how to buy and wear clothes. If she'd seen Becker's earrings, she probably would have called the fashion police. They must be going to a wedding, thought Emily as she watched Mr. Muldoon open the car door for his wife. It'd be one of those kinds that didn't allow children because the bride had spent thousands of dollars and didn't want anyone wrecking her big day.

As soon as their parents drove away, Eric and Nate ditched their rakes and disappeared into the house just long enough to put the stereo speakers on the windowsills and crank up the music. A few minutes later, their brother Joe and two carloads of his friends showed up to play basketball. The game was just getting started when a green van with New York plates finally drove up the Racines' driveway.

Perfect timing, thought Emily, and stood up slowly, her

bottom numb from sitting on the brick steps so long. Her eyes searched the van as it slowly rolled past her—parents up front; one, two, three girls in the back. They'd brought the whole family. For a second her mind raced backward, trying to remember their name—Johnson; that was it.

Mr. Johnson got out of the van, but the others stayed put. "Is this 260?" he called over to Emily.

"Excuse me?" she said, putting a hand to her ear, pretending that the music from the Muldoons' was too loud for her to hear the question.

"Is this 260?" he repeated, a little louder, as he walked toward her. "I didn't see a number or a 'For Sale' sign, but this house fits the description I was given."

Emily shook her head with disgust. "The numbers on our lamppost must be missing again. Some kids don't have much to do." She glanced in the direction of the Muldoons', adding, "If their father wasn't a lawyer, he'd go broke keeping those delinquents out of jail. My mother can't wait to move so I can have some decent kids my age to play with."

Mr. Johnson turned and looked at the Muldoons' house, where Led Zeppelin was blaring out the windows, and Joe and his basketball friends were battling it out in a game of five on four. "How many kids do they have?" he asked.

"Too many, and all boys," Emily answered. "I've been waiting so long for you to get here, I thought you found out we lived next to them and decided not to come."

Mr. Johnson choked out a laugh. "No, no, we just had a little trouble finding the place." He turned and waved at his wife and kids to get out of the van, then gave another wary glance over at the house across the way. "All boys, huh?"

"Yeah," said Emily, following his stare. "And the kids you see over there are only some of them. Eric and his hippie friends must be inside. I don't see Nate, either. He's probably up in his room spying on us with his father's binoculars, or hiding in our pool bushes again."

She let Mr. Johnson chew on that and turned her attention to the rest of his family. They might have had some trouble finding her house, but from the fleece jackets they were wearing she could tell they hadn't had a problem finding L. L. Bean. All three of the daughters were tall, willowy, red-headed, and freckled. "Hi. I'm Emily."

"It's nice to meet you," said Mrs. Johnson, who looked just like her daughters, though maybe a hundred pounds heavier. "I'm so glad we finally found your house. It's absolutely beautiful."

"From the outside, anyway," Emily agreed.

Mrs. Johnson cocked her head like she'd just heard something she wasn't sure of, and Emily took advantage of the pause. "Boy, the Muldoon brothers are going to love living next door to you girls. Are you models?"

Two of the girls smiled at her, but their older sister was already smiling at something else—the basketball game across the way.

"I hope we haven't inconvenienced your parents," said Mrs. Johnson. "We would have been here on time if my husband had stopped and asked for directions."

"Oh, that's okay," Emily assured her. "My mom's not going

anywhere; she's sick. Besides, my dad will understand; he's like that, too. When he's going the wrong way he won't stop until he finds the perfect driveway to turn around in. It's a man thing. Right?" she asked Mr. Johnson.

Silence.

Must not have heard me, thought Emily. He was too busy watching his daughter watch Joe and his friends. Come on, Joe, foul that Kenny boy, he loves to fight.

"What's the matter with you?" asked Mrs. Johnson, giving her husband a little nudge with her elbow.

"I'll tell you later," Emily heard him say under his breath.

Mrs. Johnson seemed to catch some of her husband's drift. "Do your neighbors always play their music so loud?" she asked.

"Yeah," said Emily, "but we're used to it. The only time it bothers us is when they have a party and it shakes the pictures off the wall, but that only happens on the weekends when their parents are out of town. Come on; I'll take you inside. I think Ms. Becker's probably done cleaning our kitchen for us by now."

The real-estate agent began the Johnsons' tour in the living room, where she'd managed to undo some of Emily's handiwork. The morning newspaper Emily had spread out on the floor had disappeared, and all the throw pillows she'd scattered had been neatly restored to the couch. She cleans faster than Janey, thought Emily.

"As you can see, the house faces south," said Loretta, gracefully waving a hand toward the windows, "so the sunlight in here is just divine."

And on this bright fall day Emily was glad it was. From where she was standing she could see the smudges on the glass, their rainbow sheen as pretty to her as oil in a puddle.

As though she'd just noticed those rainbows on the windows, too, Loretta quickly changed the subject. "And look at the intricate molding on that mantel. You don't see fireplaces like that anymore. And it's completely functional, as is the one in the dining room and the one in the family room in the basement. To me there's nothing more intimate or lovely than a fire on a cold, snowy night. Don't you agree?"

Mrs. Johnson nodded, but Emily noticed her husband seemed more interested in the windows than the fireplace. While Loretta was giving her spiel, he'd edged his way over to have a better look at the view.

Tugging at his elbow, Emily whispered, "The really nice thing about our house facing south is we can always tell what the Muldoons are up to. That's why we don't even have a TV in here; we just watch them."

"And I can't think of a more perfect spot for a Christmas tree than right there," sighed Loretta.

Emily followed Mrs. Johnson's dreamy stare, and her heart sank. That was where they'd always put their tree—she and Jon fighting over who'd get to put the angel on top; her father meticulously checking all the strings of lights for any frays or burnt-out bulbs, her mother unwrapping the ornaments and telling stories about when and where they'd bought each one.

"Yes," Mrs. Johnson agreed. "The perfect place."

Hot chocolate, popcorn, Jon dancing around with reindeer antlers on his head. The nostalgic feeling of those memories touched a nerve, and suddenly Emily felt a real hatred for these people standing in her living room.

"With this wonderfully high ceiling and all that marvelous space, why, you could have a tree that would put Martha Stewart's to shame," cooed Loretta.

Emily wanted them to leave. Wanted to tell that real-estate agent, "Get out of my house and take these people and your lousy adjectives with you!" Instead, she bit down on her lip.

As Ms. Becker led the Johnsons through the downstairs rooms of her house, Emily's anger followed like a shadow. Who *were* these people? Who'd given them permission to trespass into her home and her life? And where was her family when she needed them? Her mother sick in her room, her brother stuck in the cellar, her father out hiding in the Palace like a scaredy-cat. "Go out and play," he'd told her, "I don't want you bothering Ms. Becker while she's showing those people the house." Forget that! Stick to the plan, she told herself, and while Becker the Home Wrecker droned on about the chandelier in the dining room, Emily zeroed in on the youngest daughter, whom she'd been using like a shield to hide behind. "Do you have to wear uniforms where you go to school?" she whispered up at her.

The girl frowned. "No way."

"Boy, you're lucky. We have to here. They're really ugly, and the jumpers can't be more than an inch above your knee."

"Jumpers? You're kidding, right?"

"Think I'd lie about something as important as that? I can't wait to get out of this school district," Emily told her softly. "I can't take seven more years of wearing plaid."

"Plaid?"

"Yeah," said Emily, with a solemn look on her face. "Fashion crime, isn't it?"

The girl quickly turned to her sisters and relayed the awful news.

"Not in this century," said the middle daughter. "I'll stay and live with Grandma Lin first."

"And right through here," said Loretta, "is a pantry that leads to the kitchen, which gives your maid easy access while you're entertaining dinner guests. Just look at those built-in cabinets. All that extra storage space for the china and glassware you don't use on a regular basis. And those drawers beneath are perfect for storing your good silver and table linens."

"My mother's good silver got stolen last year," Emily whispered to Mr. Johnson. "The police never caught the burglars, but we have our suspicions."

"A woman must have designed this house," Loretta rambled on. "No man would have thought of storage details like this."

"I hope she wanted a downstairs bathroom, too," Mrs. Johnson said, laughing. "I'm sorry, but I had two cups of coffee this morning and shouldn't have."

Loretta tittered like she and Mrs. Johnson were best friends. "No need to apologize, Nancy; I'm the same way. Actually, this house has three bathrooms, and with three teenage daughters, I don't have to tell you that's a necessity."

Up until now, Emily had been careful to stay out of Becker's sight and hearing distance. Being so little, she'd found it easy to hide among all those tall people and quietly tell her lies. But suddenly Emily was front and center. "I can show her where the bathroom is for you, Ms. Becker," she offered politely.

The real-estate agent looked down at Emily with mild surprise. "Why, thank you, darlin'. And please bring her to the kitchen afterward, would you? That's where we'll be."

As Mrs. Johnson followed her into the main hall, Emily told her, "You'll have to use the bathroom down here, because the toilet in mine's broken and my mom might still be using hers. She has that awful virus that's going around the OR. She said the scrubs and nurses are dropping like flies. That's the one bad thing about being a surgeon; you get exposed to a lot of diseases. You never know what you might catch, especially if you get cut with a scalpel or jabbed with a dirty needle or . . ."

Mrs. Johnson cut her off. "I get the idea," she said. "I don't mean to be rude, but I'm really squeamish. I have to call Irene if the girls get a nosebleed."

"Irene?"

"She's my next-door neighbor," Mrs. Johnson explained. "I'm really going to miss her."

"If you buy our house, you'll have Mrs. Muldoon next door to help you. She has all boys, so she's used to seeing blood. Besides, she doesn't have anything better to do than lie around all day in her bikini. It'd be good for her to have a friend besides my dad. There's the bathroom. I'll wait right here for you."

It was a short wait.

Good old Jon and his oatmeal-in-the-toilet trick. "Boy, you're faster than my father," said Emily.

Mrs. Johnson's face was almost as red as her hair. "False alarm," she said. "I don't need to use your bathroom. I *didn't* use it," she added emphatically, as though she wanted Emily to know that whatever was floating in that toilet bowl didn't belong to her.

"That happens," said Emily. "Come on, I'll show you where the kitchen is."

"Ta-daa!" Emily pranced down the cellar stairs. When she reached the last step, she threw her arms in the air like Mary Katherine Gallagher and shouted, "Super Staaar!"

Smiling and using the big-screen TV for her focal spot, she pirouetted her way across the floor, her arms moving gracefully, her quick, whirling turns finally ending about an inch from the couch. "Think that was good," she panted, "you should have seen me with the Johnsons."

She flopped down on the couch and reached for her ankle to rub out the pain. "I figured they were going to come down here so you'd at least get to see them, but after going upstairs, Mr. Johnson just wanted to get out of here. 'I'll be up front with you, Ms. Becker. We're on a tight schedule, and we'd really like to see the other two houses you had lined up for us before we head back to New York. We've seen enough of this one to know it's not right for us.' "

Emily laughed at the memory. "Becker lost that plastic smile of hers for at least twenty seconds. 'That's not a problem at all, Ben; I'll just let the owner know we're finished, and you can follow me to the next house.' I think Dad's right: maybe I should be an actress. But I'd want to write the script myself." She paused, then added thoughtfully, "After I wrote the book, of course. Like Dad says, a movie's never as good as a book."

Emily got up from the couch and, pretending she was Ms. Becker, strutted her way toward the barre. "'Why, d-a-r-lin', with these wonderfully high ceilings and all this mah-velous space,' blah, blah, blah. You should have heard her go on. She's a pretty good actress herself."

Taking hold of the barre, she began stretching out while watching her reflection in the mirror. "I wish you could have been there, but, knowing you, you wouldn't have been able to keep a straight face when Mrs. Johnson touched that jelly on the banister. What a riot. She kept wiping her hand on her pants the whole time we were upstairs, then, when her daughter asked to use the bathroom, she yelled at her, 'Just hold it, Margaret; we're not going to be here long.'

"But Mr. Johnson was the funniest. I had him thinking the Muldoons were a bunch of hoodlums, and that Nate was a Peeping Tom. After the kitchen, while Home Wrecker was showing them the pool, I walked around the deck pretending I was scouting out the bushes, and when no one was looking, I winked at Mr. Johnson and told him, 'Just checking for you-know-who.' And then, when we were up in my room and his daughters were whispering about the wallpaper and saying stuff like 'I'm not getting stuck with this one,' I got Mr. Johnson again. Told him, 'If we take our blinds, you'd better buy some shades for those windows.' Like Dad always says, know your character's worst fear and your story will be believable."

What'd you tell him about my room?

Emily saw her smile in the mirror turn into a straight line. It had bothered her to watch those people walk into his room. She didn't want them to go in there, didn't want them to see or touch her brother's things. "Nothing," she said, her grip on the wooden barre a little tighter. "I didn't have to; I'd already won by then. Dad couldn't have pegged them any better than I did."

That was the term her father used while they were people-watching in the square downtown, or at the mall, or her favorite—Old Orchard Beach in the summertime. "Peg that one," he would say, and they'd take turns making things up, like the other night, while they were waiting in the express line at Shop 'N Save, her father buying two six-packs of Molson, she a new notebook for school.

"Businessman; buys his suits at Joseph's," her father had whispered.

Then it was her turn. "Keeps looking at his watch; he's in a hurry, has a plane to catch to France, just needed to pick up toothpaste. He's thinking, 'Can't you read, lady?!' "

"Yeah," her father agreed, because there was a woman in front of the man with two kids and a cartload of groceries in the Ten Items or Less line. "But that woman doesn't care what he's thinking, or if she has twenty items instead of ten, because her ice cream's melting and her kids are whining, and she just wants to get out of this store as fast as she can."

They'd played until the man paid for his toothpaste and left. And after, as they'd walked through the parking lot, the evening air feeling more like winter than fall, her father had queried her on the details: "What kind of watch? What color suit?" And the usual: "What's his worst fear?" It was a game she loved to play and was good at: Rolex; pepper-colored; that someday he might be poor and have to buy his clothes at "Wally's World," her father's name for Wal-Mart.

Emily returned her attention to her brother. "I knew the mother wouldn't want to live next door to anyone who could wear a bikini and might steal her husband, but I hadn't pegged her for being squeamish till I started telling her about Mom being sick. I was just lucky she was the one who needed to use the bathroom. I used your oatmeal-in-the-toilet trick. Worked so good, I'll have to use it again."

She did a series of pliés, then thought of something else that made her giggle. "Tell me the truth, did you peek out the window to see how pretty their daughters were? Ah, come on, I know you did. I bet you wouldn't mind them having slumber parties down here. I think that was the only truthful thing I said about the Muldoon brothers—they would have loved living next door to those girls."

Thinking of the lies she'd told about the Muldoons made her feel a twinge of guilt, but she quickly shrugged it off with one of her father's sayings, "All's fair in love and war."

seven

EMILY'S BROTHER had once told her that no matter how big he got he was never going to give up trick-or-treating. So it didn't seem fair to her that the one year Jon could be a *real* ghost for Halloween he couldn't go with her.

"Why not?" she asked him again as she checked out her costume in the mirror. Written in gold fabric-paint on the lapel of her black cape was the name Hermione, and across its back, HOGWARTS SCHOOL. "You could go if you wanted to. On that show about the ghosts at Gettysburg they said spirits were walking all over the place."

I already told you I can't, so stop asking. I have to stay here. I can't leave until . . .

"Until what?" she asked, straightening her black wizard-hat that had gold satin moons and stars.

I don't know that, either. What else did they say on that show?

"Wish I knew," said Emily. "I didn't even get to watch it till the first commercial, because Janey changed the station. She said that garbage would rot my brains out and give me bad dreams. You know how Janey is about scary stuff—she won't even watch *Casper.*"

Emily looked down at the black plastic cauldron she was going to use to collect her treats in instead of the usual pillowcase. "Just think of the cool things we could do to scare the cousins. You could whisper 'Boo!' in their ears and stuff like 'Give Emily all your Twix bars.'"

Every year she and Jon went trick-or-treating with their cousins in South Portland, whose close-knit neighborhood had small yards and a lot of houses. It'd become a tradition. Cousins from both sides of her family would meet at her aunt and uncle's house on Evans Street at about five for pizza. After supper, picture taking, and trips to the bathroom, all the kids would race through the neighborhood together while their parents tagged along in the middle of the residential street, talking and occasionally calling out things like "Slow down!" or "Car!" or "Not that house, kids, the lights aren't on!"

You'd better get going. Dad will be down here looking for you.

"Probably," she said, but studied herself once more in the mirror. Her brother had always liked to go as scary things; he'd been Dracula, and a werewolf, and last year that Jason guy with the white mask who liked to kill people with chain saws in movies her parents wouldn't allow them to watch. But Emily always chose to dress up like a character from a book she admired. Although she usually didn't care for science-fiction or fantasy novels, she loved the Harry Potter series. They were fun and made her want to believe that a world like that could exist; made her wish she could be Hermione, who was so smart and serious about her studies. If she were Hermione, she'd be able to discover some herbal potion or long-forgotten spell that would bring Jon back to life, or at least allow him to go trick-or-treating with her.

She stared down at her black-painted fingernails and her sparkly gold wand, her excitement tinged with the guilt of having to go without him. "I promise I'll save all my Snickers bars for you," she told him. Then she picked up her wand and cauldron and walked up the stairs and, with a lump in her throat, closed the door behind her.

"Did you have fun?" her father asked later that night, as he and Emily were driving home from her cousins' house.

"Everybody loved my costume," she answered from the back seat. Even the old people, who'd probably never heard of Harry Potter, knew she was a wizard and not a witch. "I got a lot of compliments."

"And a lot of candy," her father pointed out. "We'll have to go through it when we get home."

In the dim glow of the passing streetlights, Emily could see the plastic cauldron sitting on the seat beside her. "Let's check out the loot" is what Jon would have said. She closed her eyes and pictured it clearly—the two of them dumping their candy on the living-room floor, then sorting and trading it. He'd give her his Milky Ways for her Snickers, and she'd give him her peanut M&M's and Almond Joys for his Jolly Ranchers. They'd dicker: "Give you this Hershey for that Twix," and so on. Apples or anything that wasn't wrapped they'd throw away, because every Halloween Janey warned them, "Don't you kids be eatin' any apples anybody gives you. There's some sickos out there that'll put razor blades in 'em. One bite could cut your mouth wide open. And throw away anything homemade, like cookies or brownies; might be drugs in them. You just never know. Even in a nice neighborhood like your cousins' you have to be careful."

Now, from behind the wheel, her father gave her a warning of his own: "Just don't eat too much of it tonight, Em."

"I won't," she said, and knew that'd be an easy promise to keep. She'd felt so guilty eating that one Twix bar that she didn't even want to look at the rest of her candy.

"You don't want to get sick," cautioned her father.

Maybe she'd just give it all to Janey, who wasn't on a diet this week because it was Halloween. "I'll have Janey go through it tomorrow—I'm too tired tonight."

"If you can wait until then, you must be tired," said her father, and then, with more concern, he asked, "How's your leg? You did a lot of walking and running tonight."

"It feels like the bone's burning," she answered truthfully. That last street, she'd barely been able to keep up with Jamie, who was only three. But despite the pain, she'd kept on going. She knew her aunts and uncles would make their kids cut things short if she couldn't keep up, and she didn't want to spoil things for them.

"We'll have to put some ice on it when we get home," said her father. "And get some Tylenol into you."

The only thing she wanted to do when they got home was

sneak down-cellar and check on Jon. She figured he'd need some cheering up. She would have if she'd missed out on trick-or-treating with the cousins. And suddenly she felt that sharp pang again that didn't come from her leg but from somewhere inside her heart. It was a terrifying feeling that made it hard for her to breathe, a sadness that seemed to suck the air right out of her lungs. It always came without warning, and she'd already felt it more than once tonight. First, while her father was taking pictures of her in her costume before they'd left home. "Smile," he'd told her, and that's when it'd hit her—she'd be the only one in the picture this year. No Jon beside her with fingers raised like horns behind her head, no Jon dressed up like Dracula, pretending to bite her neck.

Later, while she was racing through the dark toward another lighted house—her cousins slightly ahead of her, her father, aunts, and uncles tagging behind in the middle of the street—that stab of sadness had hit her again. It was her uncle's question, "Who's missing?" that had stopped her in her tracks, and after counting heads, her cousin Ben's answer, "No one," that had knocked the wind right out of her. In all the fun and excitement she'd somehow forgotten that someone *was* missing. That painful reminder was all it had taken to trigger the suffocating feeling in her chest. It left her winded, empty, and full of guilt as she tried to keep up on that last street that had seemed to take forever.

Now, as she sat in the back seat, that panicky feeling took hold of her once again. Jon would want to know everything, and she knew his first question would be the same one she'd ask if she hadn't been able to go: Did anybody miss me?

"Jamie was cute as a Hershey Kiss," said her father, as he turned onto their road. "When you were her age, your mom wanted you to go as an M&M, but you wouldn't hear of it. You told us someone might try to eat you if you were an M&M."

She'd heard the story about Jon wanting to be a devil and Janey saying he didn't need a costume, but she'd never heard this one before. "That's a new story."

"Seeing Jamie tonight reminded me of it. Seeing all you kids together . . ."

Her father's voice sounded strange to her, as though there were tears in it.

"You're all just growing up so fast. Like your aunt said, before we know it you kids won't even want to go trick-or-treating with us anymore."

Until tonight, that was something Emily couldn't even fathom. "Guess it's like Santa," she told him. "One year you're young enough to believe in him, and the next you're too old."

"Good analogy," said her father. "Just don't get too old on me too fast."

"I'll try not to," Emily told him, but at the moment she was feeling older than her adopted grandparent Esther, who was fond of telling her, "I'm older than wooden teeth."

"And the little one's Jamie; she went as a Hershey Kiss."

"But where are you?" asked Dr. Radke, looking down at the Halloween picture Emily had drawn of her cousins.

Emily's finger slid to the left edge of the paper. "That's my foot. The rest of me's out of the picture. By the last street I was having a hard time keeping up."

"Because of your leg?"

"Mmm."

"Did you ask them to slow down?"

"Oh, they would have if I'd asked them to," Emily said defensively. "My cousins and me are like best friends. I just didn't want to ruin their fun."

"That's very thoughtful of you, Emily, but sometimes you have to think about yourself, too." Dr. Radke held up the drawing and studied it, a frown of concentration wrinkling her forehead. "You know, that you only drew your foot in the picture tells me something. Makes me wonder if you were feeling a little left out of the fun. Am I right?"

"I had fun," said Emily. At least she did until she'd remembered about Jon. By the end, she'd just wanted to get it over with and go home—she wouldn't have told her cousins to slow down no matter how much it'd hurt her to keep up. "But next year I'm just going to go to my gram's and help her pass out candy."

"Why is that?" asked Dr. Radke.

"I'm getting too old for trick-or-treating," Emily told her. "Some kids in my class didn't even go this year."

"I see," said the doctor, as though she'd just thought of something. "Emily? Was this the first time you'd ever gone without your brother?"

Emily looked down at her hands and nodded. He had to stay home in the cellar.

Covering Emily's hand with her own, Dr. Radke told her,

"That must have been hard for you. I bet you missed having him there."

Trick-or-treat, smell my feet, give me something good to eat—missed him saying that. Missed him so bad I couldn't even eat my candy.

"I'm guessing it just wasn't the same."

It wasn't, and that's just what I told him.

"Is that why you'd rather go to your gram's next year?"

It'd be too sad going without him again.

"Instead of going out with your cousins?"

Emily stared down at the painted fingernails, suddenly aware of the doctor's touch. "No," she said, pulling her hand away. "I mean, you don't go trick-or-treating anymore, do you?"

Dr. Radke chuckled. "I think I'm a little old for that."

"That's exactly how I feel. I think Halloween's like wearing snow pants to school—it's something you grow out of. The only thing I'm not sure of is how to break the news to my father. You know how parents are—he's still putting money under my pillow when I lose a tooth. But I have a whole year before I have to worry about that, so can we talk about something else? I'm bored of Halloween."

Leaning back in her chair, Dr. Radke pressed her hands together as though she were about to say a prayer. It was a habit of hers, one that told Emily something was up. When Dr. Radke put her hands together like that, a "How do you feel?" question usually followed. "Actually, I did want to talk to you about something your mother told me. She said they've put your house up for sale, and I was wondering how you felt about that?"

Emily shrugged like it didn't matter, but a tingling of fear was rushing through her. Maybe they're starting to suspect me, she thought. Maybe the couple with the two little kids and the baby on the way said something.

That family had come to look at the house on Saturday, and Emily had managed to get them alone long enough to tell them a few white lies. The parents had been easy to peg. She'd told them, "Ever since the man who got out of prison moved in down the street, I can't even play outside by myself. Janey's too afraid I might get kidnapped like that other little girl." That had gotten their attention in a hurry. "Things are so bad," she'd told them, "my dad had to take me to my cousins' to go trick-or-treating. Where they live, you don't have to worry about sickos giving out brownies with drugs in them, or apples with razor blades."

Or maybe, thought Emily, as she avoided Dr. Radke's eyes, it was the rich old man she'd gotten rid of yesterday.

Mr. Nelson was looking for a house for his daughter, who'd gotten divorced and was moving back to Maine with her children. Despite his shiny Cadillac and expensive-looking clothes, Emily could tell right away he didn't like spending money, so scaring him off had been a cinch. "My dad wants to buy land and build 'cause he says an old house will nickel-and-dime you to death," she'd told him. "Last summer the gutters, this week the water heater. And you should see our deck—our maid, Janey, has to say a 'Hail Mary' every time she walks across it so she doesn't fall through. Her cousin Mickey built it for us, and he's not much brighter than a sixty-watt bulb. Even I know you're supposed to use pressure-treated wood. He's the one who fixed our roof, too, that's why we have to keep wastebaskets up in the attic to catch the rain." Every time she told him something like this on the sly, she could see the dollar signs in his eyes and hear the *ca-ching ca-ching* as he'd added up all those costs in his brain.

Shrugging her shoulders just like Emily had a moment ago, Dr. Radke now asked, "Can you give me a little more than that?"

No, Emily decided, it wouldn't be Mr. Nelson. Although he'd been polite enough to go on Becker's tour, he'd barely asked a question about the house and never even mentioned the roof. He'd just wanted to get out of there as fast as he could so he could start looking for some cheap land in Buxton or Scarborough or someplace like that.

Dr. Radke tried again. "You know, Emily, anything you say in this room is just between you and me. I don't discuss our conversations with your parents or Janey—not with anyone. Perhaps you didn't understand that when I tried to explain it before."

"Then how come you can tell me what my mother says?"

"Because your mother's not my patient, and what she told me wasn't said in confidence, which means I can share it with you."

"Oh," said Emily. "So what else did my mother tell you?"

"That she and your father want to find a house in the same school district, which I was very glad to hear. And she explained some of her reasons for wanting to move. But my main concern is you, Emily. You've been through so much already—losing your brother, your physical injuries—you haven't even had time to heal. The idea of another change right now worries me. Moving from a familiar place, a house you've always lived in, is a big change under any circumstances."

She doesn't want them to sell the house! "Did you tell my mother that?"

"More or less. She was very understanding of my misgivings, but she assured me that you'd been part of the decision."

Yeah, right, thought Emily. The only reason they told me was because I was sick and they couldn't ship me off to Gram's.

"And perhaps I'm making a mountain out of a molehill," said Dr. Radke, tapping her pen on the desk. "I just wanted to hear for myself how you felt about it."

But telling the truth was a risk Emily couldn't take. Stick to the plan, she told herself firmly. "I want to move. I want to live in a neighborhood where there are kids my age. Without Jon, there's no one for me to play with anymore, not even my dog. She died, too."

"Thank you for sharing that with me, Emily."

"Her name was Sage, and my dad had to have the vet put her to sleep."

"I'm so sorry. I know just how you feel."

Seeing tears welling up in the doctor's eyes, Emily asked softly, "What's the matter, Dr. Radke?"

The tears were now spilling down the doctor's cheeks, and she held up her finger as if to say, Just give me a minute.

Emily snapped out a couple of tissues from the pretty flowered Kleenex box that always sat on the desk, and, leaning forward, handed them to Dr. Radke.

"Thank you," sniffed the doctor, then dabbed at her eyes and her running mascara.

Both concerned and a little frightened, Emily wasn't sure what to say. "Would you like to share?" she asked.

"I'm sorry, Emily. I didn't mean for that to happen. It's just—I lost my Irish setter on Saturday. He was hit by a car."

Hesitantly, Emily reached out her hand and lightly patted the doctor's wrist. "It's okay for you to cry, Dr. Radke. That's nothing you have to tell me you're sorry for. It's been almost four years, and I still cry when I think about Sagey."

For a moment Dr. Radke seemed to weep a little harder, and Emily pushed the Kleenex box across the desk so she could reach it. "Hurts awful when your best pal dies," Emily said, and stared up at the window that was now black. Hurts even more when it's your brother, she thought. And again that familiar feeling took hold, that painful sadness that made her feel like she was underwater and struggling toward the surface for a breath of air. She had to get out of this room, needed to get away from Dr. Radke, who didn't want her to move; who understood what it meant to lose a dog like Sagey. If she didn't leave right now, one of her secrets might slip out.

"Well," said Dr. Radke when she was done blowing her nose, "I feel a lot better." Then she gave Emily a sheepish grin. "And I'm supposed to be the doctor. I shouldn't even charge for today's session."

"Oh, don't worry about that," Emily told her. "Janey says my parents are loaded. But if it would make you feel better, you could let me go home early today."

"Nice try," said Dr. Radke, and both of them laughed.

"Still, you might want to wash your face before you see the next kid," Emily warned, running a finger across her cheek. "You have some black stuff right here."

"Thanks," said the doctor, then glanced down at her watch. "My goodness—our time's already over."

"See you next week, then," said Emily, already out of her chair and headed for the door.

"Wait," Dr. Radke told her.

Keeping her hand on the doorknob, Emily gave a concerned look over her shoulder. "What?" she asked. "Did you want to talk about your dog some more?"

Dr. Radke smiled. "Actually, I think our dogs would be a good thing for us to talk about again. But what I wanted to tell you was, I think we did some good work here today."

Emily held the doctor's kind stare for a second. "Yeah," she said, I'm glad you didn't want me to move. "I feel better, too."

eight

THE FRIGID mid-December air pinched her nostrils as Emily glared at the Becker and Brook Realtors sign at the end of her driveway. The sign was forest green with gold lettering and was suspended on silver chains attached to a white post that looked like an upside-down "L." Cautiously she scanned the road in both directions for traffic: her school bus, any neighbors out walking their dogs, Mrs. Petrie, who liked to run every morning even when the weather was bad. The coast clear, she took hold of the sign by its bottom and, leaning it against her torso, lifted it up just enough to rock it free from the two metal S-hooks. The wooden sign fell away from her and hit the frozen ground with a solid thud.

Brushing the frosty evidence off her parka and mittens, she told herself, "I'm getting good at this." Still, she couldn't take credit for the idea. The first time the sign had fallen off those S-hooks, the wind had done it. Now it was a daily topic of conversation in her house. "The wind blew the sign down again," her mother would say, and her father would answer, "You'd think, with the money that woman's going to make off us, she'd give us one that wouldn't fall off every time a breeze comes through," or "If it happens again, I'll saw the whole thing up and use it for firewood." Sometimes her father got so mad at the sign that he'd let it stay on the ground for a few days before he bothered to hang it back up. Emily figured her dad, whom Janey called "The King of Signs," was starting to hate that Becker sign more than she did.

Emily picked up her backpack and the Christmas bag with Esther's gift in it, and walked across the frosty grass, feeling it crunch like cornflakes beneath her shoes, the daily dread of riding the school bus setting in. Being the last kid picked up in the morning always made it difficult for her to find a seat. She hated having to ask anyone to move over, hated the way kids ignored her as she walked down the aisle searching, and those hurtful whispers she sometimes overheard: "Doesn't she own any clothes that aren't black?" "She's so snobby, she don't talk to no one." "Ever see her without her nose in a book?" "Thinks she's special 'cause her dad was in *People* magazine." "Quick, put your backpack on the seat so she can't sit with us."

But today, to her surprise and relief, the bus wasn't crowded at all. As she slid into one of the empty green seats near the back, the rare luxury of having one all to herself lifted her spirits and made her thankful for the flu that was going around school.

When the bus lurched forward, she turned and stared out the window. The green sign looked black against the white frost. The square grew smaller, then finally disappeared into the curve of the road. That's that, she thought, and pulled out *To Kill a Mockingbird* to see what Boo Radley was up to. She was loving this book and would have stayed up all night to finish it if the batteries in her flashlight hadn't died around 2 A.M. She'd almost found the place where she'd left off when Howie Baines, who was in her class and whom all the kids called "Brains," interrupted her.

"Hey, Emily," he whined from across the aisle.

Great, thought Emily, first time I get my own seat in forever and it has to be across from him. She didn't like Howie, mostly because he thought he was smarter than she was, and partly because when it came to math he was. She kept her eyes on her book, hoping that if she just ignored him he'd bug somebody else.

It was too much to hope for. Stretching his leg across the aisle, Howie tapped the edge of her seat with the toe of his shoe. "What'd you get your grandparent?" he wanted to know, nodding at the pretty gift bag sitting beside her.

No matter what she'd gotten Esther, Howie would make the gift he'd gotten for his adopted grandparent sound better. That's the way Howie was about everything, especially when it came to grades on tests. Knowing that, Emily just rolled her eyes and shrugged.

"I bought mine a genuine miniature replica of a World War II B-17 bomber plane."

"That's nice," said Emily, and then looked back down at her book.

"If it wasn't already wrapped, I'd show it to you," Howie

told her, his whiny voice now tinged with excitement. "My grandparent's going to love it. All he ever talks about is being a pilot and the air strikes over Europe after Normandy. Actually, I think that era's the only part of his life he remembers. Of course I had to go over the limit to purchase it, but as I pointed out to Mother, what can you buy for five dollars these days?"

Some peace and quiet? wondered Emily. She'd gladly give Howie five bucks just to shut up.

"My father wasn't too happy about it, though. He thinks Miss Parker should concentrate on academics instead of all this community-service stuff. I mean, it's not like we get a grade in it or anything, and . . ."

Emily couldn't take any more. "If you don't mind, Howie, I'm trying to read."

"Oh. Sorry," he said, but managed to slip in a dig just to remind her who he thought was smarter: "Good book. I read it last year."

Emily wanted to slap that superior look right off his face. Instead, she turned her back on Howie and edged her way as close to the window as she could. Although she acted like she was reading, concentrating on her book was now useless. Suddenly the nice-smelling bath-and-body lotion she'd bought down at Rite Aid for Esther seemed like a stupid, thoughtless gift.

Later that morning, the first thing Emily noticed when her class trooped into the community room at Pleasant Oaks was the large, fake Christmas tree. The second thing she noticed was that Esther wasn't there. As her classmates sought out their adoptive grandparents among the wheelchairs, tables, and couches, she glanced around the big room that was decorated with silver garlands and gaudy paper bells, thinking she'd just overlooked Esther's withered face and wispy white hair. But she hadn't.

She's never missed a visit before, thought Emily, but, then, neither had Fred's adoptive grandparent until he'd died of a heart attack. Esther was ninety-four—why else wouldn't she come to the party? Fearing the worst, Emily stood there by herself, trying to fight back the tears until one of the nurses finally noticed her.

"What's the matter, honey?" asked the woman, whose name tag read "Susan Peters, R.N."

Staring down at the gift bag in her hand, Emily answered in a whisper, "Mine's not here."

"Oh, I see," said the nurse, and then, scanning the room, added, "You must be Esther's."

Emily nodded. Until now she hadn't realized how fond of Esther she'd become, and despite her effort not to cry, tears started to escape.

"Well, if Mohammed won't come to the mountain, we'll just bring the mountain to Mohammed," the nurse told her. Taking Emily's hand, she guided her out of the room, where old and young voices were laughing and talking while "Silent Night" played in the background.

"Where are we going?" Emily asked as they walked past the front desk to the elevators.

"I'm taking you to see Esther," the nurse told her, then

pushed the up button. "It will do her some good. She always gets depressed around the holidays. If she'd been on my floor today, I would have made her come down."

"She's still alive?" Emily asked, her voice cracking.

The nurse laughed. "Are you kidding? That one's so ornery, she'll outlive me."

Good to know that, thought Emily. She didn't want Esther to die like Fred's adoptive grandparent. Fred now had to share one—who drooled and could hardly talk—with Danny, another boy in her class.

The elevator doors opened, and Emily followed the nurse inside. Although she wanted to give Esther her present and was curious to see where the old woman lived, she was afraid she might get in trouble. "I didn't know we could go to their rooms," she said.

"It's a lot easier for us to have you kids visit downstairs," the nurse told her. "But sometimes we make exceptions, and your teacher doesn't have a problem with that. I'll let her know where you are when I go back down."

A minute later, Emily was ushered into a room on the third floor where all the pictures and cards she'd made for her adopted grandparent were tacked to a wall.

"You have a visitor, Esther," the nurse announced.

Esther, who was sitting in a chair and staring out the window, answered, "Go away. You have the wrong room."

The nurse chuckled. "You know what I like about you?"

"Absolutely nothing," the old woman answered.

"That's right." The nurse laughed. She fluffed up a pillow and placed it behind Esther's back, and then, taking a comb from the nightstand, said, "Let me pretty you up so you don't look so scary."

Esther turned her head to protest, but when she saw Emily standing by the bed, she stayed still and allowed the nurse to fix her hair. "I'm sorry, Emmy. If I'd known this battle-ax was going to drag you up here, I would have made myself presentable."

Emily was just glad Esther wasn't dead. "That's okay," she told her.

After straightening the collar on Esther's robe, the nurse seemed satisfied. "There, you look ten years younger. Now, try to be nice." She turned and winked at Emily. "I'll be back in about twenty minutes," she told her. "If you need anything or don't want to stay that long, just press that button right there and a nurse will come."

When the nurse left, Esther adjusted her glasses with her knobby fingers. "Not much to look at, is it?"

Emily glanced around the small room. Despite the pretty curtains and bedspread, and the collection of framed, faded photographs lined up along a shelf, it looked like a hospital room: the same kind of floor, same kind of bed, same smell.

"It's nice," said Emily, though she'd hated all hospital rooms she'd had to stay in—the noises, the smell, everything about them.

"I should have gone downstairs like the others," Esther admitted. "But I wasn't up for a party or listening to 'Jingle Bells.'"

"I don't want to hear Christmas music, either," said Emily. No one in her house did. They hadn't even gotten their tree yet, and Christmas was only ten days away. Usually her mother had the house decorated by now—evergreen arrangements in all the vases; garlands with red berries and a string of white lights snaking up the banister in the hall; all the Christmas knickknacks set in just the right places to transform their house into something magical. But this year no one was into it. Her father, who was a stickler about the outside lights and religiously put them up the day after Thanksgiving, hadn't even seemed to notice that theirs was the only house in the neighborhood whose lights weren't up, or that the Halloween pumpkins had molded and collapsed into mushy piles on their front steps.

"When you've outlived all of your family, Emmy, Christmas is just another day on the calendar that you don't want to remember."

Emily looked into those blue eyes that used to scare her. Yeah, she thought, who cares about Christmas when your brother isn't there to make gingerbread houses or open presents with? Thanksgiving had been bad enough. Her mother had cooked all morning—stuffed Cornish hens, twice-baked potatoes, baby peas, sweet white corn, spinach salad, homemade rolls, cinnamon-apple pie. Her mother had worked so hard to make everything perfect—setting the dining-room table with the Royal Albert china and crystal glasses and the silverware that rarely came out of its velvet-lined wooden box. But when the three of them had finally sat down to eat, her mother had burst into tears, sobbing, "I forgot to make gravy."

"I know what you mean," Emily now told Esther. She knew it wasn't forgetting to make the gravy that had made her mother cry like that, it was remembering that Jon was the only one who liked it.

"Come have a seat," Esther told her. "You can watch the squirrels with me. I might not be able to read without a magnifying glass, Emmy, but I can still see pretty good far away. I like to watch those little rascals until it's time for *Judge Judy*—that's my favorite show, you know."

"My gram likes to watch her, too," said Emily, dragging a chair over to the window beside Esther. "When *Judge Judy*'s on she won't even answer the phone unless it rings during a commercial."

"Don't blame her," said Esther. "But I don't have to worry about that—my phone never rings."

When Emily sat down and saw the view from the window it surprised her. Harmony Lane was a narrow side street that connected the two main roads into town. It was also a shortcut to the ball fields, and the way her parents had always taken Jon to his practices and games. Although the cemetery across the street was a familiar sight to her, she'd never seen it from this height before, or thought about its location. As she looked at it now, it didn't seem right to her that they'd built an old folks' home across the street from a cemetery, or that the only view from Esther's room at the back of the building was gravestones. Glad we're Catholic, she thought. Although she hadn't seen her brother's grave yet, she knew there weren't any houses or old folks' homes next to Calvary Cemetery, because their dad used to take them there to visit Grampa.

"I've only seen one squirrel today," said Esther, "and he didn't have any of his friends with him. See that big chestnut tree? That's their favorite place to play."

Calvary was bigger and prettier and had a pond, but it still wasn't a place she'd want to look at day after day, especially if she were ninety-four like Esther. "I wouldn't want to live right next to a cemetery."

Esther smiled. "It makes for quiet neighbors," she said. "Besides, it's a comfort knowing my next stop's just across the street."

"That's awful," said Emily.

Esther laughed at her reaction. "Don't be looking so sad, Emmy. Death isn't something I'm afraid of. Why, I haven't been scared of that since I buried my oldest boy."

"When did he die?" asked Emily.

"Too many years ago to remember. I already told you, the reason I wanted a boy from your school was because I had three sons and didn't know anything about girls. Well, William was my first, and he was something special. They say you're not supposed to have favorites when you're a mother, but that was something I couldn't help. God, could that boy make me laugh. When he was killed in the war, it just about killed me, too." Esther sighed and looked back out the window.

Emily followed her gaze, thinking about Jon being her mother's favorite. Maybe Mom can't help it, either, she thought.

"Those were black days," said Esther, shaking her head. "There's no preparing for pain like that. Doesn't matter if they're sixty-six like Henry or eighteen like William—no mother ever expects to bury a child."

Turning her head, Emily looked past Esther, her eyes running along the shelf full of worn frames and old photographs until they settled on a boy in a uniform.

"But you're too young to understand any of that."

I wish I were, thought Emily, but she told Esther, "No, I'm not. On March 19th, my brother was killed in a car accident." The feel of those words in her mouth almost choked her. It was the first time she'd ever had to say that out loud—the teachers, the kids, everybody in town already knew.

"I didn't know," said Esther. "I'm so sorry, Emmy."

Still staring at the photograph of Esther's favorite, Emily told her, "Thanks," and, for once, it seemed like the right thing to say.

"What was his name?"

"Jon. Without the 'h.'"

"Pull your chair up a little closer, Emmy, and tell me all about him."

As the school bus pulled out of the Pleasant Oaks parking lot, Emily stared out the window, thinking about Esther. She'd made a big deal about the bath-and-body lotion, and an even bigger deal about the card Emily had made to go along with it. "Mine's the best wall on the whole floor," Esther had told her. "All the old ladies up here are jealous they didn't get you. You make such pretty pictures and write such lovely things." But to Emily it seemed sad that the only thing Esther had hanging on her walls was some kid's lousy artwork and sappy cards. Pleasant Oaks, she thought—what a joke that name is. Who'd want to live in a place where the only thing you had to look forward to was watching squirrels and *Judge Judy* and moving across the street to a cemetery?

Their previous visits had always been in the community room, where there were lots of people and projects to do, so she'd never seen that lonely side of Esther's life before. She'd been so caught up in her own pain that it had never dawned on her—until she'd walked into that depressing room that looked and smelled like a hospital; until she'd seen the view from that window and the boy in that faded photograph—just how lucky she was. She still had her father and mother and Gram and all her aunts and uncles and cousins and Janey, still had Jon's spirit living in the cellar. The only things Esther had left were faded pictures in a room where the phone never rang.

"So what!" whined Howie Baines. "My adoptive grandparent has a bad heart, plus diabetes."

"He's still not as bad as mine," countered Mark. "Mine doesn't have any toes on his right foot, and his cataracts are so bad he's just about blind."

Emily turned and looked at the boys behind her, who didn't have a clue, who'd never lost a brother, never had to suffer that kind of loneliness that lived in Esther's room—who saw only missing toes and cataracts.

"Mine's outlived all her family," she told them, "and there's nothin' worse than that." She narrowed her angry eyes at Howie as though daring him to contradict her. "Think about that on Christmas morning, when you're opening up your toys."

nine

ON THE LAST DAY of school before Christmas vacation, Emily's father was waiting for her in his truck at the end of the driveway. When she got off the bus, she went over to the driver's-side window, expecting him to tell her he was going somewhere, but instead he told her, "Hop in. It's about time we got ourselves a Christmas tree."

For a long moment she just looked at him, and then at the truck she hadn't ridden in since the accident because it didn't have a back seat.

"It'll be all right," he promised, aware of her fear of being a passenger up front, knowing how, if she were with Janey or him or her mother, she always sat in the back because she felt safer.

"Can't we take the car?" Emily asked, the apprehension inside her growing—sitting in the back seat had saved her life, and sitting in the front had killed her brother.

"We need to take the truck in order to get the tree," her father explained gently.

I don't want to go, then, she wanted to tell him, but something in his eyes stopped her. Getting the tree had always been a big family event—her parents wandering up and down the rows searching for just the right one while she and Jon ran wild over the snow or muddy ground at Hilltop Tree Farm, crazy with the excitement of being outside in the country, of being with both of their parents, of each getting a turn at sawing down the Christmas tree they would take home.

"Okay," she told her father, not because she wanted to go, but because she'd read that desperate look in his eyes and understood this was something he couldn't do alone. Taking a deep breath, she walked around to the other side of the truck, noticing that he still hadn't bothered to hang the Realtor's sign back up; it'd been lying on the ground for days.

She'd forgotten how high up the truck was compared with the car, and her heart felt like it was pounding in her throat as she slid her backpack across the floor's rubber mat.

"Be careful," her father told her as she began to climb into the cab, which smelled of coffee and wet gloves. By the time she'd fastened her seatbelt as tightly as it would go, her whole body was trembling and her hands inside her woolen mittens were shaking.

"Are you cold?" her father asked, flicking the heater button to high.

Although her teeth were chattering, she shook her head no—she wasn't cold, just scared to death.

"How'd school go?" her father asked, putting the truck into gear and slowly pulling out onto the road.

"Good," said Emily, staring straight ahead at the radio, too afraid to look any higher. Last week, when Dr. Radke had asked her to draw a picture of something that really scared her, Emily had taken a crayon and colored the white piece of paper completely black. When she was finished and Dr. Radke asked her to share, she'd told her, "Black ice." But if Dr. Radke, whom she'd slowly come to trust, were sitting here right now in the front seat of her father's truck, Emily would draw her a different picture. She'd draw the truck's windshield, which seemed so big and wide and close it was making her dizzy, making her remember the other one that had shattered, its glass sparkling like diamonds in the brilliant light of the rescue vehicles as she lay pinned in the back seat listening to the tapping of the freezing rain, to the last gurgling sounds of blood inside her brother's throat, to the sounds of help that had come too late to save him.

"You okay, Em?" asked her father.

It was the same question he'd repeated over and over that night when her voice was too frozen to answer, when her broken body hurt too much to move, when all she'd had to hang on to was the beauty of that shattered glass while her brother was dying in the front seat.

"You're looking awfully pale." Her father took a hand off the wheel and placed it on her forehead. "You're clammy, too."

"I get carsick sitting in the front," she whispered, as if she were pleading guilty to a crime.

“Maybe, instead of driving all the way out to Hilltop Farm, we should just buy a tree at the fire station,” he suggested. “Besides, it’d probably be too dark to see by the time we got all the way over there.”

“Yeah,” she agreed, because Hilltop Farm was miles away and the fire station barely two she could make it that far without puking, couldn’t she?

“And the money they make goes to the rescue unit,” her father eagerly pointed out, as if the prospect of Hilltop were too much for him, too. “We’d be giving to a good cause.”

“If you’re on the couch, move out of the way—I need to lie down.” Emily stretched her body across the cold, soft leather and, kicking off her shoes, let out a groan.

What’s the matter?

“This Christmas stuff is killing me. Going to get that stupid tree with Dad in the truck was awful.” She’d kept seeing things, flashes of stuff she hadn’t remembered. It’d been like watching a scary movie through that windshield. Her parents had lied to her. They’d told her Jon had died instantly—but she’d heard him; those noises in his throat. “I’m sorry,” she told him.

For what?

“For thinking that glass was pretty,” she said, bursting into tears. The ride to the fire station had brought back more than the memory of the shattered glass; it had brought back something that had been said: “We’ve got a live one in the back, but the kid in front bought it on the windshield.”

Pressing her lips against the wet leather, she buried her face in the couch, her whole body rigid and shoulders shaking with each sob. All the emotions she'd fought so hard to keep hidden from her father—who'd needed her, who couldn't have made that trip alone—now unleashed themselves in the safety of her cellar. The fear of the ride, the guilt and sorrow of the memories it had induced, raked through her like invisible claws. "I'm sorry," she repeated.

It's okay. It's not your fault.

She felt the weight of a hand on her shoulder and a cool breeze on the back of her sweaty neck, his presence calming her, his forgiving words stilling the guilt until only anger was left. "I hate you for dying," she whispered. "I miss you so bad it hurts."

Don't worry—everything's going to be all right. Don't worry—everything's going to be all right. Don't worry . . . circled through her tired brain like a comforting prayer, relaxing her body, soothing the pain, lulling her to sleep.

"Wake up there, China Doll," said Janey, gently shaking her. "Your mom's home. Time to decorate the tree."

Emily opened her eyes a crack and, still hazy with sleep, told the maid, "It's not my fault."

"What are you talkin' 'bout?" asked Janey.

"He said everything's going to be all right."

Janey gave Emily another shake. "Wake up, Em; you're still dreamin'."

Emily opened her eyes wider and, looking up at Janey, felt a jolt of panic. "Did you shut the door?" she asked, scrambling to a sitting position.

"Take it easy, China Doll. Course I did—your father's got me trained better than you kids. You know what a booger he is about that. Gives him a heart attack to see a door open."

My door's closed for a reason; didn't you see the sign? Shut that door; I'm trying to think!

Emily giggled and glanced over at the pool table.

Don't forget to close the door. Who left that door open? You kids think I'm heating the outside?

Emily was really laughing now, and when Janey asked her, "What's so funny?" the fact that it was Jon made Emily crack up even more.

Janey sat down beside her and, slipping an arm around Emily's shoulders, gave her a squeeze. "That's a good sound to hear in this house again," the maid told her. "A lot better than the noise your father was making upstairs. You should have heard him trying to get that crooked tree to stand straight—used the Lord's name more times than a priest on Sunday."

Emily relaxed in the crook of Janey's arm. If it weren't for Janey they probably wouldn't have gotten a tree at all. Emily had been eavesdropping on the back stairs as usual when she'd caught that conversation.

"I know where you and Theresa are coming from," Janey had told Emily's father. "No fa-la-la spirit knockin' on my door this year, either. But it's Em we need to be thinkin' about. How's she gonna feel walkin' in that living room Christmas mornin' with no tree, or even one of them ugly point-setter plants? Some memory that'd be of the first Christmas her brother's stockin' ain't hangin' on the fireplace."

"Does the tree look that bad?" Emily now asked. Her dad had seemed lost without her mom there to tell him which one was tall enough or full enough, and though she'd felt sorry for him, she wasn't any help. The first tree he pulled out and said, "What about this one, Em?" she'd told him, "Looks great, Dad; let's get it," because she'd just barfed up lunch in the bathroom of the gas station next door and couldn't care less.

"Throw some lights on it and a bunch of decorations, be as good as Rockefeller Center's," said Janey, shivering. "Brrr—this cellar's too cold for me. Look, I've got goose bumps the size of watermelons. Think that thermostat's on the blink. Cranked it up to seventy the other day, when I was cleaning down here, and it's still colder than Alaska."

Jingle Bells, Batman smells, Robin laid an egg . . .

Janey glanced over her shoulder, a wary look in her eyes.

The Batmobile lost a wheel and the Joker got away!

"Did you hear something?" Emily asked, her heart starting to race. Could Janey hear Jon singing his favorite Christmas song, too? Was it possible?

"Na," said Janey with a slight shudder. "Just a weird, heebie-jeebie feeling. You know, like someone's watching you but no one's there?"

"Maybe someone *is* watching," said Emily, and felt the sudden urge to confess who it was, to tell Janey, Don't worry, it's just Jon.

Better not, little sister; she'll think you're crackers, won't let you come down here anymore.

"You been watchin' that *Scariest Places on Earth* show again?" Janey scolded.

"No," said Emily, but she had been reading every ghost and haunted house book she could get her hands on at the library and had learned that some spirits couldn't move on until their business on earth was finished. Like "The Woman in White," whose spirit roams Spangler's Spring, still waiting for the lover who broke his promise to her; or "La Llorona," whose spirit is still looking for her lost child in Mexico; or the young girl from Indiana, whose name Emily couldn't remember, who'd been killed in a car accident and whose spirit keeps trying to thumb her way home though she's been dead for over thirty years. Emily wasn't sure why Jon had "stayed behind," as one book put it, but figured it was like the author said: some spirits don't want to leave their familiar surroundings or the houses they'd lived in all their lives.

"Are you fibbin' to me 'bout watchin' that scary show?" asked Janey. "You're lookin' awful guilty."

"I wouldn't lie to you," Emily told her. "I was just thinking about those twins. You know, the ones I had to tell our house was haunted just to make them behave?"

Janey started laughing. "From what your daddy said, a good swat on the bottom was what they really needed."

"That's for sure," Emily agreed. She was also sure those bratty little boys—who thought living with a ghost would be "cool" until she showed them the scars on her leg—had given their parents an earful on the way home. But she'd covered her bases. She'd told her father and Ms. Becker, "I had to tell them something to keep them from wrecking the cellar. If I hadn't made up that ghost, the little monsters probably would have smashed the TV and the computer with those pool sticks." The thing was, Home Wrecker was so grateful she hadn't had to deal with those kids while she'd been showing the house to their parents, she'd slipped Emily a five-dollar bill when she left.

"C'mon," said Janey, giving Emily's knee a pat. "You have a tree needs decoratin'."

ten

WHILE EMILY had been taking her nap down-cellar, her father had been busy. The living room was littered with boxes of decorations and ornaments. Strings of lights lay across the floor, their tiny bulbs sprinkling colored light over the carpet—all tested, ready to go.

"I don't care," he was telling her mother. "We can use the new lights you bought if you want to. Doesn't matter to me."

"I just thought a change might be nice," her mother said, an edge in her voice. "Something different."

Emily felt the tension between her parents as soon as she walked into the room. Decorating the tree, like going to Hilltop to buy it, had always been a family thing—her parents, she, and Jon. Still, looking up at Janey, she asked, almost pleaded, "You're going to stay and help us, aren't you?"

"Sure I will," said Janey, though she'd never helped them before. "No place special I have to be."

Emily's mother looked up from the shopping bag she was rummaging through, relief and gratitude spreading across her face. "Thanks," she told Janey. "We could use the help. The real-estate agent's bringing someone to look at the house at seven."

Emily couldn't believe it. Not while we're decorating the tree, Mom! No wonder Dad looks like he's ready to blow. How could you?

As though reading Emily's mind, her mother told her defensively, "I'm sorry, honey, but the woman works; it was the only time she could come."

"I didn't say *anything*," Emily snapped.

Her mother gave her one of those grocery-store stares: We're in public; behave! "I've already gotten the third degree from your father, Emily, I don't need it from you, too."

"Another Kodak moment," her father said sarcastically.

With a sharp look, her mother warned, "That's enough, Michael."

But her father wasn't through. "Welcome to *The Waltons*—anyone wanna buy our house?"

Emily knew her parents' anger was about to erupt, saw her mother's hand already reaching for the nearest thing—a Christmas ornament. The shiny red ball seemed to sail through the air in slow motion, narrowly missing her father's head, then exploded against the wall in a plume of red glass.

"Now look what you made me do!" her mother screamed at him.

"Oh, that's my fault, too?" he said, his brown eyes snapping, accusing. "Just like everything else! The house, the tree, the accident."

Janey tugged at Emily's arm. "Let's go in the kitchen," she whispered.

Emily shrugged her off. That was the ornament Jon had made in Cub Scouts.

"I never blamed you for that, Michael. Don't you dare try to pin that guilt on me. I have enough of my own, thank you."

Now it was broken, smashed to smithereens. But where was the picture? Where had it landed? On hands and knees, Emily crawled across the carpet, bits of glass biting into her palms and bare feet, her eyes searching the floor, the scattered pieces of red, the strings of colored lights. Where was it?

"Be careful, Emily!" her father shouted. "There's glass everywhere!"

"What is she doing? Stop her, Michael, before she cuts herself."

But it was too late for that. Already pinpricks of blood were welling up on the hand reaching for the one piece that hadn't shattered, its jagged surface a shiny silver on the inside. She gently turned it over, and the smiling face of her brother looked up at her, part of his painted message—"Merry Christmas 1995"—still intact.

Sitting back on her heels, Emily held it up for her parents to see. "It was his Cub Scout one," she told them.

"Not that one," moaned her mother. "Not the one he made?" She lifted it from Emily's hand and stared at it as though she couldn't believe what she'd done.

Gone were the angry voices, but the room's silence was more deafening to Emily—her mother standing above her, cradling that piece of broken glass to her chest as though it were an infant, her body slowly rocking back and forth.

"Where was I when he needed me?" her mother asked, tears dripping from her pale and suddenly weary face. "Doing a ruptured spleen. Saving some kid's life whose name I can't even remember while my own son was dying in the seat where I *should* have been. That's what I've got to live with, Michael," she sobbed, sinking to her knees.

Emily wanted to touch her, wanted to tell her mother what Jon had told her: *It's not your fault. . . . Don't worry—everything's going to be all right.* But something held her back—the feeling that she was seeing her mother naked. During that moment of hesitation, her father's arms protectively encircled her mother's shoulders, and Emily turned away.

Janey scooped her up off the floor and carried her from the room, telling her calmly, "Your parents need to be alone for a while."

In the kitchen, Emily let the maid gently wash away the smears of blood with peroxide, the cool liquid bubbling and turning brown.

"Looks worse than it is," said Janey. "Nothin' a couple of Band-Aids won't fix. Hold still, now. There's a splinter of glass still in there; I can see it."

Emily stared down at her palm, then at the tweezers in Janey's hand. "Can't my mom do it?"

"Your mother needs to take care of her own wounds right now."

Emily looked away from her hand, toward the kitchen door and beyond, her mind replaying that scene in the living room. It had frightened her to see her mother that way, looking so old and sounding so different. Her mother—who was always so strong and in control, who saved lives for a living and almost never cried—sobbing like an injured animal, crumpled on the floor like she'd been beaten.

"There," said Janey. "I got it. Don't need to be a surgeon to take out splinters."

"I didn't even feel it," Emily admitted, then studied Janey, who was still working on her hand, now applying a dab of ointment, then a Band-Aid. You're the only one in my house that's still the same, she thought, the only one who can fix us. She reached up, put her arms around the maid's neck, and hugged her. "Thanks, Janey," for staying, for not leaving me alone. "I love you."

"Right back atcha, China Doll."

Their embrace was interrupted by the sound of the doorbell.

"Great, that's all they need," said Janey. "You stay right here, Em. I'll be back in a minute."

But as soon as Janey left the kitchen, Emily followed her. The living room was empty; her parents were gone. Upstairs? she wondered. She leaned against the wall so Janey couldn't see her, heard the front door open, then Home Wrecker's voice. "Good evening, I'm Ms. Becker, and this is Wanda Poore Whitten. Theresa and Michael are expecting us."

"They were," said Janey. "But right now's not a good time for them."

"Excuse me?" said Loretta. "I don't think we've ever met."

"I'm Janey. Their housekeeper."

"Well, Janey, I talked to Theresa this morning and . . ."

"Sorry, but there's been a death in the family we didn't expect."

"Oh, how terrible," said Loretta. "Was it a relative? Someone close?"

"Yes, it was," Janey told her. "So it'd be better if you waited until after the holidays before you haul anyone over here again."

"Absolutely," said Loretta. "And, please, give the Racines my condolences."

"I'll do that. Good night, now."

Emily came out of hiding as soon as Janey closed the door. "Good thinking." You're better at getting rid of them than I am.

"You weren't supposed to be listenin'," Janey told her, a smile tugging at her lips. "I'll have to go to confession for that one."

"Sometimes you have to lie to tell the truth," Emily reassured her. "Be more of a sin if you didn't."

Janey shook her head. "You're growin' up too fast."

For a moment they just stood there staring at the mess in the living room, Emily's stomach growling for supper and her head aching.

"Let's surprise your mom," said Janey. "We'll decorate the tree; get this place all cleaned up. Be one less thing she'll have to do."

The chance to do something that might make her mother feel better gave Emily a second wind. "You get the vacuum; I'll get my shoes. We'll meet back here."

Janey vacuumed up the broken glass. Emily re-coiled the strings of colored lights and put them back in their boxes. Together they decorated the tree, first with the all-white lights her mother had bought, then the ornaments, Emily reminiscing with Janey as they worked.

"Mom bought this one when we were in New York," said Emily, hanging a miniature Empire State Building on a branch. "We had to wait in line for a year, but it was neat seeing the city from the top of the building. Felt just like I was part of the sky."

"I'm surprised you can remember that. You couldn't have been more than five when your family went on that trip."

"I was six," Emily told her, "and I remember everything. Ellis Island, with all those pictures, and stories you could listen to on telephones; the pretty jewelry in Tiffany's, where Mom bought her bracelet; and especially seeing *Swan Lake*." Watching that performance had convinced her that the only thing she wanted to be when she grew up was a ballerina. Sitting in the dark theater, watching the magic on that stage, she'd promised herself that someday she would dance the parts of Odette and Odile, and that her parents and Janey and Jon would fly all the way to New York just to watch her.

Emily tapped the ornament lightly, watched the tree lights shimmer in its silver. "I'll never forget us going on the subway, that's for sure." They'd just gotten off the boat that had taken them to Ellis Island and the Statue of Liberty. Her mom wanted to catch a cab, but her dad wanted to take the subway so they'd know what it was like. It'd been the first time she and Jon had ever ridden one, and they'd thought it was cool—until they got off and their parents didn't.

"That's one story I don't want to remember," Janey told her, placing a crystal icicle near the top. "Makes me sick to think what could have happened to you kids."

Emily and Jon had gotten out, but the door on the subway train had closed before their parents had a chance to. It'd happened so fast. One second Emily was walking out the door, the next she saw her dad trying to pry it open with his hands, her mom in the window motioning for her and Jon to get back away from the train. Then, in a blink, her parents and the train were gone, speeding away into a black tunnel, leaving them—Jon in his "I ♥ New York" tee shirt; her with that spiky green Statue of Liberty crown on her head—all by themselves.

"Two little kids from Maine, who'd never even ridden on a city bus before, on some subway platform underground, and in New York City of all places! Your poor parents were out of their minds. Your daddy said those twenty minutes aged him twenty years."

"I wasn't scared," said Emily, walking back to the table for another ornament. "But Jon was." He'd held her hand so tightly it'd hurt, and he'd kept saying, "Don't worry, they'll come get us." He'd told her, "Don't look at anyone." He'd said, "If someone talks to us, pretend you're deaf."

"You were just lucky you were with your brother and he had the sense to stay put."

"When Mom and Dad came running down the stairs and hugged us, he started bawling. But I didn't." She'd been too little then to know what could have happened to them; had, in fact, been more curious about the graffiti spray-painted on the walls, the drunk man collecting bottles out of a trash can, the people hurrying on and off the trains. She remembered it had been hot and she'd been thirsty, but she didn't remember having been scared. Jon had been with her, and she'd known he'd protect her—he always did.

"When we walked out of that tunnel place we were in Chinatown," she told Janey. "I remember there were these gross ducks with no feathers hanging by their feet in the windows, and so many people we could hardly walk. But none of them were speaking English, just a few saying, 'You buy? You buy?' And after us being under the ground all that time, I felt like I was in another world. I thought, This is what Mom must mean when she tells us at the beach, 'You dig that hole any deeper you'll end up in China.'"

Janey laughed at the story, and then shook her head as though she still couldn't let go of the other one. "If I'd been your mom, I'da been scared outta my wits."

"You kidding?" said Emily. "After that we had to take a cab everywhere that was too far to walk."

"All I can say is, God must've been sittin' on your shoulder that day."

"Wonder where He was the day Jon got killed," said Emily. "Vacation?"

Janey looked over at her, a star ornament dangling from the tip of one finger. "Good question, but it's one I can't answer. Don't know that anyone can. Drive you crazy tryin' to figure out why God lets some things happen—like them kids at Columbine, or your brother."

"Maybe He was off stopping a war somewhere," Emily offered.

"Maybe," said Janey, "but, ask me, there don't seem to be a

rhyme or reason to His plans, when you got babies starvin' in one part of the world and people eatin' out at McDonald's in another, and that's just what I told the Sisters when I took them shoppin' last Saturday."

"What'd they say?" asked Emily, curious about what the nuns, who were supposed to be married to God, might think.

"Don't get me wrong, Em, Sister Bernie and Mother are as holy as you can get, but when push comes to shove, they don't know Him any better than I do. Hand me a couple more of those icicles so I don't have to get down from the stool, will ya?"

"That looks nice, Janey. You should see it from back here. With just white lights, it reminds me of the tree in *The Little Match Girl*. I can't wait for Mom to see it."

"Well, if she don't see it tonight, she'll see it tomorrow. Think it's best if we don't bother them."

She and Janey ended up decorating the whole tree by themselves, Emily recalling as many of her mother's ornament stories as she could, pausing now and then to listen for sounds of her parents, still hopeful they might come down from their room. Janey helped her set up the hand-carved Nativity on top of the piano, where it always went, and helped her put out some of the Christmas candles and familiar figurines. In the bottom of one of the last boxes, Emily found the Christmas stockings. Fingering the reindeer on Jon's, which, like hers, had been knitted by their gram, she felt a knife-sharp pain in her stomach that made her want to cry. She stared over at the mantel above the fireplace and wondered how her mother would feel seeing it hanging there, then decided it'd be better if she didn't. She rolled it up in a ball and hid it under one of the couch pillows, thinking, I'll take it down-cellar, hang it up for him down there. And when Janey takes me shopping, she thought, I'll buy him a new CD to listen to, and a candle that smells nice, and maybe a *Sports Illustrated* so he can catch up on his favorite teams. And after they go to bed on Christmas Eve, I'll sneak down there and fill up his stocking just like Mom does. "Here are the stockings," she said, handing them to Janey.

Janey always spent Christmas morning at their house, and her stocking was on the top of the pile. "Mine's so old," she said, "it's starting to fall apart."

Emily watched as Janey hung them up on the small gold hooks above the fireplace, neither saying anything, but both aware of the empty hook where Jon's should have been. Emily was surprised Janey didn't ask where his was, but was grateful that she didn't.

"I'm not going to drag those boxes up to the attic tonight," said Janey, with a sigh. "We'll just stack them in the hall nice and neat and your daddy can take them up there tomorrow." She wiped away something from the corner of each eye and then turned her back on the fireplace. "I don't know about you, China Doll, but a pepperoni pizza and a root beer down at Angeloni's would sure hit the spot."

Anywhere would be better than being here, thought Emily. That empty hook was tearing her apart, too. Glancing over at the grandfather clock that was going to start chiming in three more minutes, she pointed out with disappointment, "It's almost nine o'clock."

"So what? There's no school tomorrow, and Angeloni's don't close till eleven. Now, here's the plan—you grab your bear and your PJs, and after pizza, we'll pick up a movie and have a slumber party at my place."

"Yes!" said Emily. "We haven't done that since . . ." Jon died.

Janey gave a nod of understanding and told her, "Yeah, so it's 'bout time we did. Just be real quiet while you get your things, and don't forget your toothbrush. I'll go leave a note for your parents in the kitchen; they won't mind you comin' with Janey. Do them good to have the whole place to themselves."

Be good for me, too, thought Emily.

And it was.

eleven

FEAR CHURNED in her stomach as Emily watched the falling snow through Dr. Radke's window. It had started right before lunch and was now coming down hard and fast. Must be four inches already, she thought, noting that some of the branches of the maple tree were starting to droop under its weight. Although she'd missed two appointments because of the holidays and really wanted to see Dr. Radke, the thought of the slippery ride home was filling her with dread. It wasn't Janey's driving that Emily didn't trust, it was the certainty that there was a patch of black ice hiding beneath the white surface just waiting for their car to come along.

She looked away from the window, stared down at the blank piece of paper on the desk. She didn't feel like drawing any pictures, but picked up a crayon anyway, the weight of it in her hand feeling like lead. When Jon was alive, snow meant building forts with tunnels, and snowball fights. It meant playing

King of the Mountain and sliding in the dark on the hill out back. They'd stay outside until their fingers felt like sticks inside their mittens, till their faces felt like they were going to fall off; even then they'd hate to call it quits. Once, she and Jon and Nate Muldoon were having so much fun making an igloo and pretending they were Eskimos living in Alaska that she'd peed in her snow pants because she'd tried to "hold it" so long. And now, like her dancing, like her brother, like the house she'd always lived in, something she loved was being taken away from her. It's not fair, she told herself, and, feeling a surge of angry determination, put the crayon to the paper and boldly printed: Black ice stole my brother but I won't let it steal the snow.

Seeing the words she'd written made it seem real, made her feel powerful. For a moment she marveled at the magic of it, how the crayon in her hand suddenly felt like a weapon.

By the time Dr. Radke came in, Emily had already written half a page and was so into it she didn't want to stop.

"Hello there, stranger."

"Be with you in a minute," Emily told her without looking up, her hand still scribbling away. Like her father always said, she was on a roll; she had to finish before she lost her train of thought. "I just have to finish this paragraph."

But that paragraph quickly led to another, and Dr. Radke and the room and the storm outside disappeared. It was only Emily and the battle inside her head, her thoughts completely focused on the words that were setting her free. She could sense the rhythm in the writing that came as easy as breathing, felt a tingle of power charging through her as she recaptured the quiet and the stillness of those tunnels they'd built out of snow. Only after she'd written enough so she could safely leave it did she remember where she was. Looking up at the doctor, who'd been patiently waiting, she said, "Now I know how my dad feels when he's 'In the Zone.'"

Dr. Radke laughed and reached out her hand. "Can I read it?"

Instinctively Emily covered the paper with her arm. Those are my words, she thought, I own them. If I share them, the magic will go away.

Although Dr. Radke withdrew her hand and said, "That's okay," Emily felt she owed her an explanation.

"My dad says that sometimes he needs to just write for himself. That's why he has a file drawer with a 'Never to Be Published' sign on it. He told me all the books he's written that came out lousy and the ones that weren't even good enough to finish live in there. He said someday he's going to burn it all so no one will ever read or try to sell it after he's dead. He calls it his 'no-one-but-me stuff.'"

Emily stared down at her arm lying across the paper, protecting that memory she'd recaptured in crayon. "This is my no-one-but-me stuff—I wouldn't even share it with God."

Dr. Radke nodded. "I certainly can respect that. I keep a journal. Writing's my way of dealing with things that bother me."

"When my dad's not writing he drinks a lot of beer," said Emily as she neatly folded the paper. "But I think he's working on a new book or something, 'cause there's been hardly any in the refrigerator since Mom wigged out, and I can hear him typing through the door again."

"Back up a moment," said the doctor. "What did you say about your mother?"

Emily hesitated. "What?"

"Wigged out?"

"Oh. That. Yeah, well, remember what I told you happened at Thanksgiving? When she started crying about the gravy?"

"I remember."

"It was like that. Only this time she broke a Christmas ornament that Jon made. It was an accident—she meant to throw it at my father, but it hit the wall instead."

"I see. I bet she felt bad about that."

"Wicked bad. She didn't know it was Jon's."

"Were they fighting when it happened?"

"Kinda."

"Would you like to talk about it?"

"I don't know," said Emily with a shrug. "That blaming stuff's pretty hard to follow if you don't live there."

"Try me."

Emily slipped the paper into her sweatshirt pocket, where it would be safe, then looked back at the doctor, whose caring eyes were still waiting for a chance to understand. "Ever blame something on one of your kids, but they weren't the ones who did it?"

Dr. Radke raised a hand as though swearing on a Bible. "Guilty," she said. "I don't think there's a parent who isn't."

"Well, it's sorta like that," Emily told her. "Like, my dad blames himself 'cause he was driving, and he thinks my mom blames him, too. But she doesn't, she thinks it's her fault, 'cause she was saving some other kid's life instead of sitting in the seat that Jon was killed in. And Janey, she blames God, 'cause He doesn't have a rhyme or reason to His plans." Emily let out a sigh. "Told you it was confusing."

"Who do you blame?"

"The black ice," Emily answered without hesitating. "But what can you do about that? Move to Florida? Then you'd have the hurricanes. And if you moved to California, you'd have all those earthquakes and fires."

"You've thought about this a lot, haven't you?"

"Some. But, the way I figure it, it doesn't matter where you are, you're going to have to live with something scary, and I think I'd rather live with black ice than tornadoes. Besides, I love the snow. I don't want to move away." I don't want to move at all, and that sad thought made her think of another. "Did you see my house in the paper?"

"No, I'm afraid I didn't. When was it in?"

"The Sunday one—yesterday's. It wasn't a very good picture, and Ms. Becker spelled two words wrong." Emily rolled her eyes and shook her head.

Dr. Radke pressed her fingers together like a steeple, a familiar gesture of hers that Emily knew meant "Listen up."

"What?" asked Emily.

"Just from some of the things you've been saying, I'm getting the feeling that you don't really want to move. Am I right?"

"If we don't, my parents will probably get divorced, or else my mother will throw a hammer next time instead of a Christmas ball." Emily forced a smile, like she was kidding, but Dr. Radke didn't laugh, just gave her that penetrating look, the one that sometimes made Emily feel like the doctor had X-ray vision and could see right through her.

"Is that what you're really afraid of, losing your parents?"

The question made her feel so uncomfortable that Emily

got up out of her seat. She wandered over to the window and looked through the darkening glass at the street below, where traffic crawled, the falling snow reflected in hazy headlights. "They took me to the cemetery."

They'd gone on Christmas Eve, had brought a basket made out of branches that her mother had filled with evergreens and silk flowers. There was a red velvet bow on the handle, and, hanging between the arms of the ribbon, a little drummer boy ornament with a place for a photo in the belly of the drum.

"They did?" Dr. Radke now asked, her thin eyebrows arching with surprise. "That was the first time you've been there, right?"

Emily nodded. It hadn't been at all like she'd pictured. She'd thought Jon would be buried under a nice shady tree, like Sagey was, instead of in the open, not a tree close enough to keep his grave out of a hot summer's sun. It'd surprised her that his stone wasn't bigger, didn't have angels on it, was pinkish-brown instead of light gray. She'd expected him to be near their grandfather, whose grave was in the older part of Calvary, where the beautiful statue of Michael the archangel stood like he was guarding all the souls, where the lily pond—in which she and Jon had once caught a frog while their father was planting flowers—lay beneath a pretty stone bridge. Whenever she'd imagined it, she'd seen sunlight and green grass and lots of flowers. But the picture in her head had been all wrong. It was freezing out, the wind whipping at them, the pewter sky spitting snow, the frozen ground dirty brown-yellow, the grass so dead she could see the edges of the rectangle that'd been made last March, while she was still in the hospital. It had made her glad she couldn't feel him there, couldn't hear his voice like she did in the cellar.

"And?" Dr. Radke asked gently.

"He's buried in the new part, where there are hardly any trees."

All the stones were so new-looking, so close together it had made her afraid of stepping on someone and made it hard to breathe as she'd watched her mother—whose eyes and nose were as red as that velvet bow—place the basket in front of his grave. Jon's picture in the drum of the drummer boy, smiling back at them like the whole thing was some kind of joke.

He was born in March and died in March and "It was weird seeing his name, you know?" said Emily. "But what was really scary was seeing my parents'."

"What do you mean?"

"Their names were there, too."

And that was what had surprised her the most. She'd never expected to see her parents' names, their birthdates cut so neatly, each followed by a dash and an empty space that had sent chills right down to her aching-cold bones.

"That *is* scary," said the doctor. "I'm sorry you weren't prepared for that."

Emily's angry gaze was still on the traffic. "They should have told me a lot of things," so I didn't have the wrong picture in my head. "Should have taken me there a long time ago."

"I can understand why you'd feel angry, Emily. He was your brother—you wanted, *needed*, to see where he was buried. But maybe your parents waited because they didn't think you were ready. Or maybe they weren't ready to take you there until now."

"I never thought of that," she admitted. "But I never knew people put their names on graves when they weren't even dead yet, either. Whoever thought up that stupid idea?"

"I take it that's not a question you asked your parents?"

How could I? thought Emily. Mom standing there, crying her eyes out; Dad staring at the ground like his mind was writing a story someplace else.

Besides, seeing their names had scared her so bad she couldn't even talk. It'd made her think of Scrooge in *A Christmas Carol* when he saw his name on the tombstone, made her realize something she hadn't been prepared to face—someday, after her parents' names and those dashes, there was going to be a date, just like Jon's. "No," she told the doctor. "I didn't dare to."

"Well, that's an important question we need to talk about. You see, it's a common thing, Emily, especially for married people who've lost a spouse and for parents who've lost a child, to have their names on a family stone. It's mostly a matter of convenience—it's easier and cheaper to have all the names engraved at the same time. But I think it's also comforting for someone who's lost their husband or wife to know that when they die they'll be buried next to that person they were married to, or, in your parents' case, beside your brother."

Emily turned away from the window and glared at the doctor, who'd been watching her the whole time. "Why wasn't my name there, then?" she demanded. "I'm part of that family, too, you know!"

"Of course you are, but . . ."

"It's not fair!" Emily slammed her fist against the thigh of her bad leg.

Dr. Radke flinched in her chair as though she'd received the blow, but said nothing.

Emily caught the doctor's startled look, but there was no turning back, no chance of her being "fine" today. "They got to do everything!" she shouted. "Got to see him, got to go to his funeral, got to pick out that dinky stone that isn't even the right color."

She began limping around the room, her hands gesturing wildly as she "shared" it all. "He's not even near the lily pond! But no one cares what I think. There's no 'Loving brother of Emily Racine' anywhere on his grave; he's just the 'Loving son of Michael and Theresa.' You can't even see Grampa or the angel statue where they put him. Hey, guess what, Jon? Mom and Dad buried you between some people we never heard of instead of next to Grampa, but don't worry, they spelled your name right, didn't put the 'h' in 'Jon.'" Emily stopped just long enough to inhale. "He doesn't even have a tree."

Exhausted, she slumped into the same chair she'd started out in, and stared up at the painting whose frame was still, *always*, slightly crooked. "You know, if you hide a tack in the bottom corner of that frame it'll stop it from tilting and driving me crazy every week."

Dr. Radke cocked her head at the painting as if seeing it for the first time. "I never noticed," she said calmly, "but thanks; I'll try that. Now, let's get back to the cemetery."

"Have Janey show you; she's an expert. Crooked pictures drive my mother insane."

"Emily."

"Last week, in the bank, she walked right behind some guy's desk just to fix one."

"Look at me."

"It's the only thing I got from her, and I don't even want it."

Dr. Radke got up and, with her back to Emily, adjusted the painting. "How's that? Is it straight?"

"Just a little to the left," Emily told her. "There. That's better, thanks."

"You're welcome."

Watching the doctor return to her seat, Emily raised her palms in a gesture of surrender. "I'm sorry," she apologized. "I know it's stupid to let crooked pictures bug me when a patch of black ice could kill me on the way home, but I can't help it. Tell you the truth, I was glad my mom fixed that one in the bank, even though I hid by the door so no one would think we were related."

"It's okay to want pictures to be straight, Emily. There's nothing wrong with that."

"I guess, but when it's not your house, people always look at you like you're nuts. The guy in the bank sure did, so my mom just told him what she always says: 'Someday, when you need to be operated on, you'll be glad I'm the one making your incision.'"

Dr. Radke chuckled and then looked back at the picture she'd just straightened. "I guess it's a good thing I didn't become a surgeon."

If you had, thought Emily, I wouldn't have anyone to talk to. There were some things she just couldn't tell Jon—like where they'd buried his body. "They should have asked me," she said. "I could have told them about the lily pond, could have told them where he'd want to be."

"Yes, you could have," Dr. Radke agreed. "But remember, you'd been seriously injured in the accident. You were in the hospital, had just gone through surgery, and . . ."

"There was a phone right by my bed," Emily interrupted. "Besides, one of them or Janey was always with me."

"But . . ."

"There's no buts about it. I never would have buried my brother next to strangers in that new part with no trees. And I would have made sure he had a huge stone with angels on it instead of a stupid pigeon with a twig in its mouth."

"You mean a dove?"

"Whatever." Emily felt the tears rolling down her cheeks, the salty taste of them in her mouth. "The least they could have done was put my name on there—they put it on my dog's."

"I can't speak for your parents," said Dr. Radke, offering Emily the box of Kleenex. "I'd only be guessing if I told you that your brother's buried in the new section because it's the only place where people can still buy a plot in that cemetery. But I can tell you why your name isn't there."

The doctor waited for Emily to blow her nose and then continued. "It's the same reason why my name isn't on my mother's grave. You see, when I die, I'm going to be buried next to my husband, so that's the stone my name will be on."

Emily thought about that for a moment. "Is that a law?" she questioned.

"No, but someday, when you grow up and get married, you'll understand why people do it that way."

"If it's not a law, then they can go ahead and put my name on there right now, 'cause I'm never getting married." Emily crossed her arms and added defiantly, "I don't even *want* a boyfriend."

"When I was your age I didn't, either," the doctor told her. "But things change. Look at me—I'm a wife and mother of three boys now. And, to be honest, some days that's still a surprise to me."

"Janey's not married," Emily pointed out. "When she dies she wants to be cremated and leave her ashes to the wind up on the Western Prom. That's what she says every time we go past a cemetery. But no one's going to burn my body up after I die, 'cause I'm going to give my heart away, like Jon did, so some other kid can still live."

"That's an amazing thing, isn't it?" asked Dr. Radke. "Being able to donate our organs when we no longer need them, to someone who does?"

"That's what my mom said when she told me about Jon. But I don't think they'd want Janey's organs." Shielding her mouth with her hand, Emily whispered, "She smokes. I wish she'd quit."

"I wish my father would, too."

"Is his name on your mother's grave?"

"Um-hmm. And, despite his cigars, he's still relatively healthy. That's why I think that, even though it's been eight years since we lost my mother, it still upsets me to see his name when I visit her grave."

"I know what you mean," Emily agreed. "It's scary 'cause someday there's going to be a date after that line."

"Exactly, but I'm hoping that won't be for a long time."

"Me, too," said Emily. She was starting to realize that it wasn't moving that terrified her the most, it was the thought of her mom and dad dying; of them leaving her all alone. "That'd be even worse than losing Jon," she admitted.

Those words were just leaving her mouth when a soft rapping came at the door. Exchanging startled looks with Dr. Radke, Emily whispered, "That was spooky."

The doctor winked at her and whispered back, "Just my secretary; we must be out of time." Then, glancing down at her watch, Dr. Radke called, "Come in, Linda."

Linda opened the door just enough to poke her head through. "Sorry to disturb you, but I thought you should know your last two appointments canceled because of the weather, and Janey's getting a little anxious to get on the road—you're already twenty minutes over."

"Tell her Emily will be out in a minute, and that I apologize for keeping her waiting."

"I will. And I'm putting on the answering service, because I'm heading home, too. It's pretty bad out there."

"Thanks, Linda. I'll see you tomorrow."

Once the secretary closed the door, Emily said with a small amount of guilt, "I didn't even ask if you had a nice Christmas."

"I didn't ask you, either," Dr. Radke pointed out. "So that's something we can talk about next time."

That'll be a short conversation, thought Emily. They didn't go to Mass; didn't go to Gram's for Christmas dinner; didn't even bother to get dressed.

Not that she'd cared. Like her parents, she hadn't felt like doing anything. So they'd just hung around the house all day in their new pajamas, reading, sleeping, watching movies together, and, from time to time, going off by themselves to cry in private—she in her room; her mother in Jon's; her dad out in the Palace. When her teacher had asked Emily and the other students in her class what their favorite Christmas present was, Emily couldn't even remember what she'd gotten. It was only when she'd vaguely answered "Books?" that she'd realized it had really been the surprise she'd heard in Esther's voice when the old woman answered the phone on Christmas morning.

"Yeah, I'd better get going," said Emily. "It's beano night. Wouldn't want Mrs. Winallthetime to get Janey's lucky chair 'cause of me." She stood up, her ankle feeling stiff and sore. After a quick glance toward the window and the storm outside, she told the doctor, "Just in case I get killed on the way home, thanks for listening and fixing the picture."

"I'm glad you told me it bothered you, and I promise I'll try that trick to keep it straight." Dr. Radke came around the desk and draped an arm around Emily's shoulder and, as they walked out together, she told her reassuringly, "Try not to worry; I'm sure Janey will get you home safe and sound."

The only one left in the waiting room was Janey, who already had her coat on and the car keys in her hand.

"I'm sorry we ran late," Dr. Radke told her.

"No problem," said Janey. "They canceled beano. A little snow and those 'Storm Center' news guys got everybody buyin' a week's worth of groceries and gettin' out their flash-lights."

Dr. Radke laughed, which of course only encouraged Janey to say more. "And that music of theirs—enough to scare you to death. Due-due-DUE-due; due-due-DUE-due. Tell me listenin' to that hasn't given some old folks a coronary before they ever got to their shovels. No kiddin', I'd like to give those weather boys a bulletin of my own: This is Maine. It snows. So, if you ain't expectin' more than a foot and a half, can the heart-attack music and lose the sweaters. Right, Doc?"

Dr. Radke, who'd been laughing all the way through the maid's monologue, said, "You're so funny, Janey. But you're definitely right."

Janey smiled, pleased with her performance. "Thanks," she said, then told Emily, "Get your coat, China Doll, it's time to cruise."

Emily walked around the corner to the coat rack, but as soon as she heard Janey ask in a serious whisper, "How's she doing?" she stopped in her tracks to listen.

"Good," Dr. Radke answered in a reassuring voice. "She's come a long way."

"She has," said Janey. "And I'll be straight with ya. I wasn't too happy 'bout her comin' here in the beginnin', but now I think it's been the best thing for her. Guess sometimes it's easier to tell your troubles to a stranger."

"There's a lot of truth in that," said Dr. Radke, "but you deserve a lot of credit, Janey. She thinks the world of you, and your being there for her through all this has been very important."

"She's like my own; been takin' care of her since the day she was born. I don't know if she told you, but her parents finally took her out to the cemetery. Been my place to, I'da taken her out there a long time ago."

Emily pulled her coat off the hanger and threw it on. Not wanting them to know she'd been listening, she hurried back around the corner. "All set?" she said sweetly.

"What took you?" asked Janey, sizing her up. "You back there listenin' to us?"

There was no fooling Janey—she knew all the tricks—but, wanting to save face, Emily tried another. "No," she lied, "you weren't talking loud enough."

Although both the adults laughed, Janey was quick to tell her, "Don't be fresh, China Doll. And button up that coat—it's freezin' outside."

"I'll see you next week," said Dr. Radke.

I hope so, thought Emily.

"Bye, Doc," said Janey. "Drive friendly."

"I will."

When Janey opened the door, a blast of cold air and a gush of snow hit Emily full in the face.

"Judas-priest," said Janey. "Maybe those weather boys were right for once."

twelve

"YOU SHOULD SEE it outside," Emily told her brother as she put on her ballet slippers. "No way there'll be school tomorrow. Took us almost an hour to get home from Dr. Radke's. Janey told Dad we could have walked home faster. Didn't tell him about the swears she said, though. Six of them—I counted. She even used the 'f' word when that idiot cut right in front of us by Captain Newick's. Think she forgot I was in the back seat, because she didn't even say, 'Pardon my French.'"

After tugging down the ends of her leggings, Emily pulled up her baggy legwarmers, her hand hesitating for just a moment on her sore ankle. "Saw a couple of cars off the road, but no bad accidents like ours. Thank you, Jesus. He must have heard me praying. Told Him if He got us home all right I wouldn't erase Home Wrecker's calls for a week."

Dumb deal.

"I know, but I was scared. So was Janey. She told Him, 'Jesus, if I get up this driveway I'm staying put.' So now she has to sleep over in the guest room tonight."

Leaning forward, Emily began to stretch out, her mind still on Janey. "Good thing she keeps some PJs here, or else she'd have to wear Dad's. No way Mom's would fit her." Especially not one of those nightgowns in her bottom drawer, thought Emily. That's where she'd found the missing medals. They were in a clear Ziploc bag, hidden beneath a layer of pretty, silky nightgowns she'd never seen her mother wear. The ribbons on Jon's gold medals for the two-hundred-meter freestyle and the hundred-meter butterfly had some brown stains on them, which Emily had figured must be blood. Cradling those medals, she'd understood why her mother had put them in a drawer where no one was supposed to look. As she'd held those ribbons to her lips and kissed them, she'd felt as if some invisible knife were slicing away another piece of him. Another piece gone, like the fading smell of his Red Sox hat that she still slept with under her pillow; or the piece she'd lost on her birthday, when she'd realized he was always going to be fourteen, that even when she was twenty, even when she was Esther's age, he'd only be that old or younger every time she closed her eyes and saw him. It'd made her wish she'd never gone looking for those medals at all. Made her mad at her mother for not hiding them better.

The sorrow and guilt of that discovery now passed through her as she warmed up her muscles, preparing her tired body for the more strenuous work ahead. "I'm just glad Mom's not on call tonight," she said, slowly rotating her head from side to side, each stretch in between starting to relax the tense muscles in the back of her neck. "Won't have to hear that stupid phone ring," which sounded louder than a fire engine in the middle of the night. "Won't have to stay awake," waiting for the headlights to flash across the picture of Mikhail Baryshnikov on her bedroom wall.

Placing herself at the barre, Emily automatically drew those imaginary lines—one running down through the center of her body and ending right between her feet, the other straight across her hips. Somewhere in the back of her mind she could hear Debbie, her ballet instructor. Long necks, ladies! Shoulders down; chest out; tummies and bottoms in!

At Christmas, Emily had decorated the cellar, taping a string of white lights along the edges of the mirror. She'd liked the effect of it, the way it was easy to pretend they were stage lights. She liked it so much that when she packed away the other things—Jon's stocking, the Santa statue, the fake tinsel tree her aunt had made for them years ago—she'd left the lights where they were. But now their brightness brought out something she didn't care to see in the mirror. "Look at me," she told Jon, scrutinizing her bloodshot eyes and the dark circles beneath them, which seemed almost blue against her chalky skin. "I look awful. No wonder Janey said I've got bags under my eyes. I do."

What do you expect? You haven't slept for three nights.

With a measure of alarm, Emily said, "If Mom doesn't stop taking call, I might grow up to be ugly. I told you she was on all weekend. Don't think there's anyone left in Portland who still has a gallbladder." Her mother had gone back and forth from that hospital like a Ping-Pong ball. "She told Dad all the drunks and loonies were out on Congress Street 'cause of the full moon, so then I had to worry about that, on top of her running out of gas and skidding off the road, and . . ."

You can't lose sleep over things you can't change, and Mom's never going to change her job, so stop whining about it.

"I can't help it." Since Jon had died, whenever the phone rang in the middle of the night Emily couldn't get back to sleep until she heard her mother come home. She'd just lie there thinking up awful things, like her mother's Mercedes coughing to a stop on Congress Street, right where a gang of drunks was fighting with broken beer bottles and guns. Or her mother racing her car past the dark woods along Highland Road and then suddenly seeing a deer caught in the headlights.

"Someone's got to worry about her," said Emily. "You know Mom. Doesn't matter to her if there's a blizzard, or if it's Christmas—nothing's going to stop her from doing a case. Not even that naked man who thought he was a dog. Remember him? The one in the doctors' parking lot that was barking at the moon? If it'd been me, I would have locked the doors and drove away as fast as I could, then called the cops on the cell phone. No way I would have ever gotten out of that car. No way I would have told him, 'Put some clothes on or you're going to catch pneumonia.' She's so used to telling people what to do she forgets to be scared."

Maybe if you were a surgeon you wouldn't have been scared, either. Mom's used to seeing naked people. Can't operate on them with their clothes on, Einstein.

"E-ew," groaned Emily. She'd never really thought about that. "Another good reason why I'm never going to *be* a surgeon. She'd better not start counting on me to do that, now that you're dead."

You? As if. You'll be a writer, like Dad.

"He sure wasn't happy about the ad Home Wrecker put in the paper," Emily giggled. In second position she did a grand plié, the heels of her feet firmly on the floor. "He didn't even finish breakfast he was so ticked off, and you know how he likes his Jimmy Dean sausage."

A misspelled word in a final draft is unacceptable!

"Wish you could have seen his face when I reminded him of that rule. 'And she has *two,* Dad—I'd fire her if I were you.'" Placing her arms in fourth position, Emily performed a rapid series of grands battements, the hair along her forehead beginning to dampen with sweat, the skin beneath her leotard starting to prickle.

Think he will?

"It might be better if he doesn't."

What?

"You were the one who was always good in math. Think about it. What are the chances of us getting another real-estate agent who's as stupid as she is?"

True.

"She's so clueless, she doesn't even suspect me." Emily extended her right arm gracefully, her palm lifting upward, her fingertips pointing with a reverent flair toward her reflection in the mirror. "She thinks I'm nothing but a sweet little girl."

Got her fooled.

"Yeah, if she weren't trying to sell our house, I could even feel sorry for her."

The snow fell all night and into the morning, canceling schools, day-care centers, Meals on Wheels—the list flashing beneath the sweater-clad newsmen on "Storm Center" seemed endless. Emily, who had jumped out of bed as soon as she'd heard their reliable plowman rumble up the driveway at 5 A.M., now sat in the kitchen, eyes glued to the TV.

The initial joy of having a day off from school started to wane as she watched live footage of an accident on Tukey's Bridge. The flatbed trailer that had jackknifed just beyond the Washington Avenue on-ramp was lying on its side, its load of lumber scattered like toothpicks. The close-up of the cab, whose front end was crushed against a concrete median, made her feel sick to her stomach. "How can you show that?" she shouted at the reporter who was now warning viewers to take an alternate route.

Emily turned her back on the TV, her anger laced with disgust. What if his family were watching? That'd be a real nice thing for his kids to see while they're trying to find out if they have school or not.

She stared down at her mother's pocketbook lying on the table. Through the blackened windows of the kitchen she could see the whirling light of the plow, still out there working on their three-hundred-foot driveway. Hearing that thumping, scraping thunder of metal as the plow rammed snow into mountains, she felt another wave of nausea. Had *their* accident been shown on TV, too? Had her mother seen what the car looked like after it'd slammed into that tree on Ruby Road? Was there a close-up of the windshield? "We've got a live one in the back, but the kid in front bought it on the windshield."

Emily looked at the screen again. A woman reporter, holding on to her jacket's fur-trimmed hood with one hand and a microphone with the other, was saying, "And as you can see, Kevin, the wind has really picked up in the last hour, making visibility a nightmare for early-morning commuters. . . ."

As she watched the coverage of the storm that had already dumped fifteen inches of snow on southern Maine, Emily's worry continued to grow. No matter how much she wished it, she knew her mother's job wasn't going to be one of the cancellations listed at the bottom of the TV screen. She'd learned early that surgeons never got a snow day off and knew all the reasons why. She'd heard them every winter since she was little. How her mother's patients had to rearrange their whole lives in order to have their operations done. How they had to take time off from work, had to find someone to take care of their kids or their pets, how they'd come in by dogsled if they had to rather than reschedule their surgeries. Although Emily was proud that her mother was a surgeon and helped save people's lives, at times like this she wished her mother was a teacher or a sales clerk at the Maine Mall, which, according to the news, wasn't going to open until noon.

During a commercial, Emily's mother strode into the kitchen like a woman on a mission, or one who was late. "Morning, Mom."

Her mother stopped moving long enough to plant a kiss on

top of her daughter's head. "You should have slept in, Em. I told you last night you wouldn't have school this morning."

"The plow woke me up," Emily explained. "But Janey's still sleeping."

"Shoot," said her mother, glancing toward the empty coffee-maker, "I forgot to set the timer." She picked up her pocketbook and started pawing through it.

"We've gotten fifteen inches already," Emily informed her mother, who was now rifling through her black briefcase.

"Great—not there, either." Her mother abandoned her briefcase, checked the counters, the junk drawer, mumbling as she went. "I told him last night I had a mastectomy at seven-thirty. 'I'll get up and shovel you out.' So where is he? Still in bed." Her mother's voice rose slightly as she ran her hand along the top of the refrigerator. "Don't ever marry a man who plays golf, Emily. Marry someone who mows the lawn and shovels."

"They say it's really bad out, Mom. Near-whiteout conditions."

"Good," her mother said, as if her mind were on something else. "Have you seen my keys?"

Emily avoided the question. "There've been all kinds of accidents. The driver that crashed his tractor trailer on Tukey's Bridge is in serious condition."

"What hospital did they take him to?"

"I don't know."

"Must need neuro or the orthopods," said her mother, "because no one's beeped me." Then, almost in the same breath, she added, "Maybe I left them in my coat."

"Maybe you shouldn't go to work today, Mom," Emily pleaded, just as a commercial ended, and the due-due-DUE-due scary music of "Storm Center" came back on.

"Don't start with me right now, Emily," her mother warned. "I don't have time for that this morning."

For a moment her mother's words seemed to hang in the air like the terrifying dirge still sounding from the TV.

"You won't have any time if you get killed," Emily desperately pointed out, her heart beating against her ribs like a hummingbird's wings. *If you die, I'll lose you for good. You could never be happy living in the cellar.* "The guys on the news said the driving's treacherous. They said everyone should stay home."

Her mother, who'd just discovered the keys weren't in her coat either, snapped, "You know that only applies to people whose jobs can wait."

"Or whose kids matter," Emily hissed back, her anger and frustration finally breaking through her fear. She'd had it. She was tired of worrying, tired of losing sleep over things she couldn't change—tired of trying. She felt her mother's hand on her shoulder and flinched as though she'd been burned.

"I promise this weekend we'll have a Mommy-Daughter Day. Okay?"

Mommy-Daughter Day, Mommy-Son Day—a day all by themselves with just their mother, who'd take them to lunch and a movie or shopping or anywhere they wanted to go. Jon used to call them "guilt days," used to say, "Start out asking for something big, something you know is way too expensive, and after that she'll buy you anything you ask for." *I don't want a Mommy-Daughter Day,* Emily wanted to tell her—*I just want* a Mommy. "I'll call your office and see if I can get an appointment," she said sarcastically.

"That's enough, Emily!"

But it wasn't. For months Dr. Radke had been coaxing her to voice her feelings, and right now Emily wanted to say something that really hurt. "I'll tell your secretary you need to schedule some *quality time* with the only kid you have left."

Her mother looked like she'd just been slapped. "Whatever happened to my sweet little girl? I don't even know you anymore."

"Why would you?" Emily said like a challenge. "You're never home anymore."

"I know I'm a lousy mother, Emily, but I'm trying the best I can. And before you say anything else, I want you to think about something besides how hard *you* have it."

Here it comes, thought Emily: how her mother had had to put herself through college and medical school, how hard she worked to give them all the things she'd never had as a kid. Well, right now, Emily didn't want to hear it.

Her mother placed a hand under Emily's chin and tilted her head back. "Look at me, Em. Do you really think I want to drive to work in this mess? Do you think you're the only one who's scared?"

Her mother? Who wasn't even afraid of a naked man howling at the moon? Who once kicked the door of a car that had almost run them over in a crosswalk so hard she'd dented it? Who'd once driven them through that slummy neighborhood in Boston so they could see the creepy, run-down building she'd lived in as an intern—the whole time acting like it was no big deal, like those narrow, scary streets were as safe as Broad Cove? Her mother scared? No, she hadn't thought about that.

"Believe me, honey, I'm terrified, because you're right—I *do* only have one kid left, and I can't stand the thought of losing her, too. Honestly, there's nothing I'd rather do this morning than stay right here in this nice warm kitchen and make pancakes for you. But I have to operate on a woman with breast cancer—the worst kind—a young mother with two little kids. How can I tell her I can't perform her surgery because it's snowing?"

Two little kids? thought Emily. "Is it the same kind that killed Becky's mom in second grade?" she asked.

Her mother nodded gravely. "And what she's facing is far worse than any storm I have to drive through. Do you understand that, honey?"

Emily pulled the keys out of the pocket of her fleece robe and placed them on the table. "Sorry," she said.

Emily figured her mother, who was staring down at the keys with a startled look on her face, was going to yell at her. But she didn't. She gave her a hug instead and told her, "I'll call you as soon as I get there, so you'll know I'm all right."

Emily didn't waste time changing into her clothes; she just ditched her bathrobe for her coat, slipped her bare feet into her boots, grabbed a pair of mittens, and headed out the door to join her mother.

In the eerie quiet that comes with falling snow, they worked together, shoveling away the bank left in front of the garage door, clearing away what the plow couldn't. Emily's feet were freezing and the blowing snow felt like sand whipping against her face, but she didn't complain, and neither did her mother, who wasn't even wearing any boots. In the shadowy light they worked quickly and with a sense of camaraderie that made Emily glad that her father hadn't gotten out of bed.

It didn't take them long to free the car from the heated garage—fifteen minutes, maybe less. Before heading down the driveway, her mother promised once again that she'd call and told her, "Thanks for helping me, Em. Go inside now and get warm."

To Emily—whose hair was matted with snow and whose ears were stinging—the suggestion was tempting. But she remained where she was, squinting through cold tears and swirling snow to watch the red taillights disappear down the dark driveway. Waited there in her rubber boots with no socks on, shivering in the icy wind, till she finally saw the Mercedes' foggy headlights go down the main road. Her mother, who was as scared as she was, driving away in near-whiteout conditions. Her mother, who'd said she was terrified of losing her, too, creeping down the snowy road, not because she wanted to, but because she had to. And as the lights vanished from Emily's view, it dawned on her just how brave her mother was.

Turning toward the house, Emily stared up at the glowing lights in the kitchen, where, seemingly just moments before, a storm of another kind had played itself out. She'll be all right, Emily told herself, then hurried inside to get warm and wait for the phone to ring.

thirteen

THE ANTICIPATION was killing her. Hurry up, thought Emily, as she waited for Dr. Radke to come in and discover the surprise that was sitting in her chair. Although she knew there was no way it could have gone anywhere, for the second time Emily sneaked a peek at the white paper bag she'd decorated with red hearts and Valentine stickers. Then, hearing that familiar click of high heels coming down the hall, she rushed back to her seat and the drawing she'd started.

Instead of going to her desk when she entered the room, Dr. Radke stopped and gave Emily's shoulders a squeeze. "I've been thinking about you all week, so don't keep me wondering another second—did you go?"

Emily answered the question by holding up the picture she hadn't finished: a drawing of herself—black swimming suit, yellow racing cap, stick arms doing the butterfly through the pool's blue water.

"Good for you!" said the doctor, punching a fist in the air in a show of victory. "Was it fun?"

Looking at her artwork, Emily nodded. Her decision to go to Becky's splash party had been a hard one, but her parents had let her make it all on her own. "I'm glad I went." It had felt so good to swim again, to be back in the water, her body so light and her foot able to move without hurting. The pain that still plagued her when she danced disappeared while she was in the pool, even when she did the dolphin kick on her butterfly—a stroke no one else at the splash party could do.

"I was the best swimmer there," she bragged to Dr. Radke, and that had been important because Becky had invited all the girls in their dance class. Emily had enjoyed showing those girls, who wore pointe shoes for part of practice every week in Debbie's studio, that she was still the best at something. "Even giving them head starts, I won every race."

"Awesome."

"Janey says swimming's like riding a bike—you never forget how to do it." And, like always, Janey had been right. Emily hadn't forgotten how to do the fly or a flip turn, hadn't forgotten the smell of chlorine, or how voices, whistles, and the sound of kickboards echoed off the tiled walls.

Walking across that deck, she'd remembered a lot of things—how she used to sit up in those sweltering stands watching her brother practice when she wasn't old enough or good enough yet to be on the team; remembered their last swim meet together, how he'd knelt on the deck near the timers in her lane so she could see him waving her on every time she took a breath on the last lap of her fifty fly; her brother cheering for her, her brother the first one to congratulate her for taking six seconds off her best time. "The only thing I forgot," Emily now told Dr. Radke, "was how much I liked it."

"I'm so proud of you," said the doctor, reaching over to push the hair out of Emily's face. "Even though we talked a lot about it last week, I wasn't sure you'd decide to go."

"Probably if my mother told me I had to I wouldn't have," Emily confessed. "I would have just told Becky I was sick or something."

"It was important that it was your decision," Dr. Radke agreed.

"And remember how I was afraid everyone would stare at my leg and stuff? You know, 'cause we always wear tights and legwarmers in ballet class, so no one's ever seen it?"

"Um-hmm," the doctor said.

"Well, Tina Noble was the only one that said something mean. She said my skin looked like melted cheese when we were changing in the locker room."

"I bet that didn't make you feel too good."

"I almost started crying. But then Becky told me, 'What do you expect from an airhead?' And then she showed me a scar she got from cutting her finger on a tuna can, and then Lindsey showed us a big one on her knee from getting her patella fixed, and Jessie had one under her bangs from her little brother hitting her in the head with a croquet mallet. So after that I didn't feel so bad, 'cause it seemed like everyone had a scar somewhere from something."

"That's right. And do you know what, Emily? Sometimes the scars we can't see are the worst."

"I know, that one under Jessie's bangs was about this long." Emily held her fingers apart. "She said she had to have twelve stitches."

"I didn't mean those kinds of scars," said Dr. Radke, and then she pointed to her chest. "I meant the ones people have on the inside after something bad has happened to them."

"Oh," said Emily, catching on. "Yeah. Even though they didn't say anything, I think it was really hard for my mom and dad. You know, being at the pool?" She wasn't the only one remembering things at Becky's splash party. Just by the way her father, who was never mushy in public, had his arm resting on her mother's shoulder, she could tell they were thinking about Jon, too. But she'd been glad both her parents had gone with her, glad they'd told Becky's dad no when he'd offered to give Emily a ride home so they wouldn't have to stay, glad that every time she'd looked up in the stands they were there watching her.

"It was a big step for all of you," said Dr. Radke. "And the ride there? How was that?"

"Just like you said it'd be."

Dr. Radke gave her a sad smile and nodded.

"On the way there, I kept my eyes closed the whole time we were on Ruby Road. But on the way back . . . something made me peek through my fingers. You can tell where we hit the tree. It's all carved up. And there's a white cross right beside it. A wooden one. I could see it coming up out of the snow."

"I know; I've driven by it."

"Mom said Janey's the one who put it there," said Emily, and felt such a powerful rush of love that the writer in her just had to embellish. "I figure she probably got it from Mother, or Sister Bernie. Probably had the priest at the scary Jesus church bless it, too, 'cause the nuns live right next door."

"How did you feel when you saw it?"

Emily thought for a moment. "That I was glad I peeked through my fingers." Even though it had made her cry, it had felt good seeing that white cross. Good to know that something—besides that scarred-up tree—was there to remind people driving down Ruby Road that her brother had died there.

"That was a very nice thing for Janey to do," said the doctor. "She has a big heart."

The word "heart" reminded Emily of her surprise. "Why don't you go ahead and sit down, Dr. Radke? I bet your feet are killing you."

"How'd you know that?"

"'Cause the first thing you always do is take off your shoes when you sit down in your chair."

Dr. Radke laughed. "That's the price I have to pay for wearing high heels, Emily—bunions." And a moment later, "What's this?"

"Look inside and see," Emily urged.

"Godiva! My favorite!"

"I know," said Emily, giving her a sly smile. "You mentioned it once."

"You have a memory like an elephant."

It was Emily's turn to laugh. "It comes in handy," she said. You should have seen me get rid of that lawyer. Emily figured whoever came up with the saying "Lawyers are all alike" knew what they were talking about: if Mr. Jordan had some hair on his bald head, he could have been Mr. Muldoon. He'd kept looking at his Rolex as though he was charging Home Wrecker by the minute, kept cutting her off as though what she had to say about the house wasn't important. But, having lived next door to the Muldoons all her life, Emily knew what would be important to a lawyer. Although Nate's dad's law practice was in Portland, he had an office in their house three times the size of her father's Palace, and she remembered Nate telling her, "This is where my dad works the other twelve hours of the day." When Ms. Becker left them to find a Kleenex, Emily had told Mr. Jordan that they lost power every time it stormed. "During the ice storm of '98, we didn't have it for almost three weeks. Going without heat and lights and having to flush the toilet with buckets of water is one thing, mister, but try to imagine living without your computer."

Mr. Jordan had stood there looking like he was thinking exactly that, the frown on his face knitting his eyebrows together into a furry caterpillar. And suddenly this man, who she could tell didn't like kids, was acting like he was her best friend. He'd asked what else was wrong with the house, and she'd managed to tell him plenty by the time Ms. Becker returned. The only problem was, Emily might have told him too much. She had a feeling he must have said something to Home Wrecker, because since that day, Ms. Becker had started showing the house only when Emily was in school.

"Here," Dr. Radke now told her, holding out the box of chocolates. "You first."

"Thanks," said Emily, taking one that didn't look like it had nuts in it.

Dr. Radke seemed like she couldn't decide which one she wanted, her pretty fingernails, a pearly gray today, hovering first over one, then another. "This was so thoughtful of you, Emily. But you're making me feel guilty."

"Why?"

"Because I know how much these cost."

Emily shrugged. "I don't mind spending a lot of money on something if it's worth it. For her birthday, I bought Esther a stained-glass star in the Old Port, and you know how much things cost down there. You should see it, it's really pretty hanging in her window. Each of its points is a different shade of blue—that's her favorite color."

"Sounds as lovely as this candy."

"Thanks," said Emily. "I figured it'd give her something to look at besides the cemetery across the street." She delicately licked her finger, savoring the last taste of melted milk chocolate, and then, lifting her eyes to Dr. Radke, she said, "Would you like to share another one?"

"Please do," the doctor told her, "or I'll end up eating the whole box myself. So much for my diet."

"Look at it this way," said Emily, "there's only half the calories when you share them."

Reaching for another piece, Dr. Radke told her, "I like the way you think, Emily."

fourteen

AT BALLET CLASS, Debbie had told them they should start thinking about their spring solos. "May will be here before you know it, ladies," she'd said. "You need to decide what music you'd like to dance to."

Emily could always use the music she'd selected last year and the dance she'd already choreographed but never had the chance to perform. That was her mother's suggestion. "And you already have the costume," her mother had pointed out. "So we wouldn't have to worry about that."

Although that seemed like the reasonable thing to do, Emily wanted to do something new, something different.

But now, as she sat in the cellar with CDs scattered everywhere, she was starting to think her mother's suggestion was a good one. "There has to be something you like," she told her brother, who didn't have a clue about ballet music or the stories they were about. They'd already listened to Tchaikovsky's music from *The Nutcracker* and *Swan Lake* and Prokofiev's *Cinderella* and *Romeo and Juliet*, as well as several selections from *The Firebird* by Stravinsky, but Jon had said *Nada* to each one.

"What about this?" she asked, putting in yet another CD. "It's about a girl named Giselle who falls in love with a prince, but he's supposed to marry someone else, so she dies of a broken heart. But then she becomes a ghost, like all the other women in the cemetery that died of broken hearts, and every night they trick men into coming into the cemetery and then kill them by dancing them to death. And then, one night, the prince she loved comes to the cemetery, and 'cause she still loves him she keeps him dancing until dawn so he can live. I saw a Russian troupe do it on PBS, and . . ."

Just play it!

But her brother didn't like Adolphe Adam's music, either. *They wouldn't have to dance me to death; listening to that music's enough to kill me. Don't you have anything with words?*

"You're hopeless," said Emily, who'd been envisioning herself as the brokenhearted Giselle, wearing a white flowing costume just like that Russian ballerina. "You don't appreciate anything."

Why don't you ask Dad, then? He's the one who likes that "soothe the savage beast" stuff.

It was true, classical music was all their father ever listened to, and his favorite joke before turning on the truck radio was, "I need something to soothe the savage beast." Although her brother would always complain about the station, Emily liked it. Before her father had built the Palace over the garage when she was five, his office was the guest bedroom right next to hers. Every night she'd gone to sleep to the music of his typing and Bach, or Mozart's *Magic Flute,* or Handel's *Messiah.* It'd taken her a long time to get used to the quiet after he'd moved out to the Palace. "You got the wrong bedroom growing up," she now told her brother. "If you'd had mine, you'd know what you're missing."

I know what I'm missing, but Dad's music's not on the top of that list.

"What is?" she asked, thinking maybe she could get it for him.

Being the next batter up with the bases loaded.

Emily looked over at the bookcases, her eyes drifting across the trophies until they settled on the picture of Jon in his baseball uniform, his blue eyes smiling back at her beneath the maroon cap, his hands proudly holding the MVP Award. But a grand slam, like the one he'd hit in the game against Augusta when his Little League team won the state championship, wasn't something she could give him, wasn't like a CD she could buy. "What else?" she asked.

Janey's cookies.

She could get some of those, but he wouldn't be able to eat them.

Dad's voice in the crowd when I'd step up on the starting block. The smell of Mom's hair. Everything outside those windows.

Staring up at one of the cellar's small rectangular windows, Emily told him, "What I miss most is seeing you."

"Em!" her mom called from the top of the stairs. "I'm ready to go."

"Be right there, Mom!" Emily yelled back.

Where you going?

"Mommy-Daughter Day," Emily explained. "But I don't know where she's taking me. She's been acting kind of weird about it, like it's some big secret. Probably the mall."

"I feel like a chauffeur," said her mother as they drove down the driveway. "You sure you don't want to sit up front with me?"

Ignoring the question, Emily asked, "Where to, James?"

"Very funny," her mother said in a tone that meant it wasn't.

"The mall?" Emily queried hopefully.

"I'm not in the mall mood," answered her mother, whose idea of shopping was to get in and out of there as fast as she could. "And I definitely don't want to eat lunch at Friendly's."

Shoot, thought Emily. Friendly's was her favorite place to eat. She always ordered the chicken-nugget dinner that came with an ice-cream sundae that looked like a clown, its hat a sugar cone, its eyes and mouth made out of M&M's. No mall, no Friendly's—some Mommy-Daughter Day this was going to be, and they weren't even out of the driveway yet. "What's the plan, then?" she asked, knowing her mom never left home without one. Her mother wasn't like her dad, who'd get in the car and take a drive just for the heck of it. "Adventures" is what he called them, because you never knew where you were going or where you'd end up or what you'd see along the way. But her mother didn't understand that kind of fun, couldn't just get in the car and drive off without a plan and a list.

"It's a surprise," said her mother, smiling at her in the rearview mirror.

Maybe she's going to buy me something, thought Emily, her

sour mood starting to lighten. Ask for something that's way too expensive and she'll buy you anything you want after that. "What kind of a surprise?"

"If I tell you it won't be one," her mother teased. "But first I wanted to show you a house that I saw for sale."

Now, there was a surprise that left Emily wordless.

"It's right on the way," her mother continued, like it was no big deal, like Emily's heart wasn't hammering inside her chest with panic. "And right on the water. Wouldn't it be nice to look out your windows and see the ocean?"

"We already live close enough to smell it," Emily quickly reminded her. Especially on foggy mornings, when the scents of salt and seaweed were so heavy in the misty air she could smell them like perfume on her clothes. "I don't need to see it to know it's there."

Staring out the car window, Emily tried to get a bearing on where they were headed. They were traveling along the back road toward Fort Williams, the ocean and stretches of rocky coast coming in and out of view between the mansions built along the water. The huge houses that would be half hidden by summer leaves seemed even larger to her through the winter-bare trees and naked sunlight. "I bet those houses are wicked expensive," she said, trying to bring her mother to her senses.

"You're right about that," her mother said, chuckling, then a minute later took a right on a dead-end street that Emily had never even known was there.

The handful of new Cape Cods along the steep, narrow street looked like dollhouses compared with the places they'd just passed on Shore Road. In the snow-covered yards, Emily spotted snowmen and flying saucers and other signs of kids, though she didn't see any outside playing.

"There it is," said her mother as they slowly drove down the hill toward the house at the very end and the winter-blue ocean just beyond it. Leaning forward in her seat, Emily stared past the Century 21 sign and the falling-down picket fence, her wary eyes taking in the shape of a house whose Victorian style was so different from the rest. It'd been built with its back to the street, its front facing the water, and its weathered gray shingles and paint-chipped trim told her it had been there for years.

"I found this the other day when I got lost," said her mother, stopping the car in front of the small driveway, which, from the looks of it, hadn't been plowed all winter. "Come on," she told Emily. "Let's check it out. I didn't have time the other day."

No way I'm getting out of this car, thought Emily, whose stomach felt like it wanted to throw up. Her mother, who never left home without a plan, had tricked her, had used their Mommy-Daughter Day like a lie just to get her to come here. "You're not supposed to do that without an appointment," she told her mother coldly.

"It's all right," her mother assured her. "I don't think anyone lives here."

And I don't want to, either, Emily almost shouted, but the expectant look on her mother's face stopped her, took her totally by surprise, for it was Jon's blue eyes that were staring back at her. A slant of sunlight caught the mischievous sparkle that Emily knew so well, the one that told her he was up to something and couldn't care less about getting into trouble.

"Okay," said Emily, because she couldn't say no, could never say no—*Come on, Em, write this paper for me.*

Reluctantly she climbed out of the warm car and slammed its door as hard as she could. Her mother could make her come, but she couldn't make her like it. "There's no garage," she said. "No place for Dad to have a Palace; no place for you to keep your car. And where would I put my bike?"

"Good point, Em," her mother answered. "Maybe I should have taken you with me to those other places."

What other places? wondered Emily. Then she realized something that made her feel even more betrayed: this wasn't the first house her mother had looked at! For a moment Emily was so numb she couldn't even move. "But we haven't sold our house yet," she said, running to catch up to her mother, who was already halfway over the snowbank.

"I know, and after seeing what's out there, that's certainly a mystery to me."

Emily almost lost her footing over that comment and would have taken a serious digger if she hadn't thrown her arms out to catch her balance.

"Be careful, Em, it's slippery," said her mother, who wasn't being careful at all. She was marching toward the gap in the picket fence as though she already owned the place.

Through knee-deep snow, Emily followed her mother's footsteps along the side of the house, barely aware of the pain in her ankle, but very aware of her guilt. It was so heavy she could hardly drag herself through the snow. All those people she'd lied to. That their house hadn't sold yet wasn't any mystery to her.

"No one buys a house in Maine in the winter, Mom! That's what Janey says." And Emily believed Janey because Home Wrecker—who was now showing their house only when Emily was in school—hadn't sold theirs yet. Like she'd told Jon, We won't have to worry about her till we see the grass again.

When she reached the front yard and saw the view, Emily had to stop to catch her breath. The snow-covered lawn gently sloped toward the water and ended in a rocky bluff maybe fifteen or twenty feet above the breaking waves. To the right was a rickety-looking set of wooden stairs that led down to the big rocks below, and a small stretch of beach where there was bound to be sea glass and shells and maybe even sand dollars.

"Isn't it beautiful, Em?"

Emily, who was already wondering if those stairs were safe enough to take her down there, glanced over at her mother. For a fleeting second in the blare of sunlight reflecting off all that snow and brilliant water, Emily didn't even recognize the person who was looking at the house instead of the ocean. Her mother's legs were half buried in the snow, the tails of her open coat flapping like wings, her gray-streaked hair blowing in the gusty wind like a wild woman's.

"I wouldn't want to be here during a hurricane," Emily shouted over the wind's roar, which seemed louder than the pounding waves.

"That's a widow's walk," her mother called back, pointing up to a small balcony above the porch. "They built those so wives could watch for their husbands' boats when they were out to sea."

"I already know that," said Emily, who'd caught up to her mother by then. "Can we go now?"

"I just want to peek in the windows first," said her mother, already trudging ahead, through the drifted snow, in the direction of the white-capped steps and the long porch that looked like it might have had screens once.

"The police are probably going to come and arrest us for trespassing," Emily warned.

But that only made her mother laugh. "If your brother were here, we'd already be upstairs looking at the bedrooms."

Emily couldn't argue with that. Knowing Jon, he wouldn't have cared if those stairs out there were safe or not; he would have gotten down to that beach one way or another, would have already been searching between those big rocks for barnacles and starfish, would have already put his hand in the water just to see how cold it was. "Don't be a scaredy-cat," he would have yelled at her. "Get down here and see what I found!"

"Yeah," agreed Emily. "He'd be out on that widow's walk lighting off firecrackers by now."

"And hoping to get in trouble just for the fun of talking his way out of it," said her mother, who was waiting for Emily on the top step, her eyes gazing past her daughter, maybe even past the ocean. "'But, Mom, I didn't steal those flowers, I borrowed them for you.'"

"You okay, Mom?" Emily asked with concern, her hand tugging on her mother's coat to get her attention, to let her know she was there.

Her mother shook her head like she was trying to stop staring at something. "I'm okay, sweetie," she said, pulling Emily against her and holding her in a tight hug. "I just really miss him."

And he really misses the smell of your hair, thought Emily, her face resting against the rough wool of her mother's coat. And Janey's cookies, and Dad's cheering, and everything outside our cellar windows. "Too bad he couldn't live here. I bet he'd like it."

"I know he would."

"I mean, who needs a pool when you've got your own ocean?"

"That's right." Her mother chuckled, and then, releasing Emily enough so she could look down at her, she said, "You'd make a good real-estate agent, Em. You know that?"

Imitating Ms. Becker's voice and body language, Emily cooed, "Darlin', where else would you ever find a house whose paint was peeling as beautifully as this?"

For the first time in a long time her mother's laughter sounded real to Emily, sounded happy.

"That was perfect," she said, her wind-red face creased with a smile. Then, holding out her hand, she told her daughter, "Come on, let's look in the windows before the police show up."

If they do, thought Emily, I'll just tell them I'm selling Girl Scout cookies. They can't arrest us for that. "Okay," she told her mother, and, hand in hand, they walked across the snowy porch.

An hour and a half later, they were driving along Shore Road again, this time toward home. Emily had been right: her mother did buy her something on their Mommy-Daughter

Day. In fact, her mother had already bought the golden-retriever puppy earlier that week, from a breeder who lived only two streets away from the house whose windows they'd peeked through.

"I can't believe it," said Emily, pulling her jacket around the puppy that was shivering in her lap. "She's so cute. I already love her!"

"Let's hope your father does. I didn't tell him about this. I didn't want to give him the chance to say no. You know how he feels about getting another dog."

Yeah, Emily knew. Her dad said he couldn't have any more dogs because he didn't ever want to put another one to sleep. After having Sagey, she didn't think she'd ever want another dog, either. "He'll change his mind," she told her mother. "I have." Then, hugging the puppy closer, she said, "Thanks a zillion-billion, Mom."

"You're welcome, honey, but you'll have to thank Dr. Radke, too. She's the one who gave me the idea."

"I will, I promise," said Emily. "And I promise I'm going to take real good care of you," she told the puppy, who was looking up at Emily as if she already knew who her best pal was going to be.

"What are you going to name her?"

Emily thought for a moment. "I don't know yet," but Jon and I will think of something. Burying her face in the soft, warm fur, Emily inhaled one of her favorite childhood scents. "Don't you just love the smell of dogs, Mom?"

Her mother smiled at her in the rearview mirror and said, "Ask me that in about a week."

fifteen

AND A WEEK was about how long it took for that new puppy to get used to Jon and stop peeing on the cellar floor every time Emily took her down there. Jon had said they should call her "Tinkle" or "Puddles" because of that, but "Sandy"—the color of the puppy's coat—was the name Emily chose in the end.

Emily had noticed right away that Sandy seemed to know Jon's spirit was living in the cellar, and at first the little golden retriever wasn't too happy about it. She'd whine and whine to go back up the stairs that she wasn't big enough to climb, or run around the room with her tail tucked between her legs like the Muldoons' nasty barn cat from next door, which the puppy was terrified of, was right on her heels.

The first time Sandy *didn't* pee on the cellar floor, Emily told her brother, "I think she's starting to like you." And with time, that seemed to be the case. Sandy no longer cowered by the steps crying to go back upstairs, no longer left a puddle on the floor as soon as Emily put her down. Instead, she seemed to be excited to be down there, wagging her tail and sniffing the floor and the air as if she, too, had just caught a whiff of Jon's hair gel. "Where is he?" Emily would ask, and the puppy would race off in one direction and then another, her paws moving so fast across the slippery tile floor that sometimes she'd slide right into the furniture. But on occasion Sandy would come to a standstill, one small paw lifted in a point, just like Sagey used to do when she was on to a groundhog or a squirrel or a bird. *The Great White Hunter*, Jon would tell Emily, and Sandy's ears would perk up as if she'd heard him.

So, a few weeks later, when Dr. Radke asked, "How's Sandy doing?" Emily's first thought was: She's not afraid of Jon anymore.

Out loud she said, "I brought you some pictures."

"Awesome! Let's see."

"Some of them didn't come out too good," said Emily, taking the photos out of an envelope. "I don't have a good camera like my dad's, but I'm saving up for one."

"Aw, she's so cute," said Dr. Radke. "Look at that sad little face."

"That's 'cause Janey was scolding her for pooping in the living room. Janey says if she finds one more doodle on that carpet, Sandy's going to be eating her dog food at the pound."

Dr. Radke laughed. "Looks like Sandy believed her."

"Must've," said Emily. "She's almost housebroken now. She's getting good at letting us know when she needs to go out. She hardly ever has an accident down-cellar anymore."

Emily flipped to the next picture: a photo of her dad and Sandy snoozing on the couch. "Mom calls that our coma couch, 'cause whenever you lie down on it you fall asleep."

"Great picture."

Imitating her father's voice, Emily said, "'I'm not going to have anything to do with that dog.' That's what my dad told my mom when we first brought Sandy home. He said, 'You bought it, Theresa; it's your responsibility, so don't be expecting me to feed it or take it to the vet.'"

Smiling at the picture, Dr. Radke said, "You'd never guess that by looking at this picture."

"Yeah, I knew he'd change his mind. By the next day he was calling Sandy 'Little Rascal.' He's bought her more toys than I have, and he's always taking her out for walks. She loves being outside. When I get home from school, that's the first thing we do. And sometimes Nate comes over and plays with us, too. He really wants a dog but his mom's allergic; that's why their cat has to live in the barn."

"Who's Nate?"

"He lives next door. I've known him forever. He used to be Jon's best friend." Nate had told her one day when they were trying to teach Sandy to shake hands that he really missed her brother. He'd said their basketball team had stunk without him, and that last year the baseball team was the same way. "He's really nice for a boy," said Emily. "And almost as smart as me."

"Then I'd say he must be very intelligent."

"He has his own telescope, a real one, and he knows everything about the planets and black holes and stuff like that. He's a lot more mature than the jerky boys in my grade." And a lot cuter, too, thought Emily, flipping to the next picture. "Here's one of Sandy barking at herself in my ballet mirror down-cellar. It's wicked funny watching her, 'cause she thinks it's another dog."

"That's a neat one. You can see you in the mirror taking the picture of her," said Dr. Radke, leaning over for a closer look. "But what's that foggy stuff behind you?"

Emily had wondered about that, too, and figured it had to be Jon. Her brother always did like having his picture taken. "They probably screwed up developing," Emily told her. "But it's still my favorite."

As they looked through the rest of the pictures, Emily gave a running commentary. After showing Dr. Radke Sandy's dog crate in the kitchen, she told her how Amy Hyland, the woman they bought Sandy from, said it was the best way to train puppies, and how Janey would tell Sandy, 'Get in your house,' whenever they needed to go shopping or somewhere else. The last picture was of Emily's mother laughing down at Sandy, who was prancing around the kitchen with a chew toy in her mouth. "Look how tiny she was," said Emily. "I can't believe how much she's grown in just a month. Dad says she's probably going to be about the same size as Sagey."

"That's a good picture of your mother," said Dr. Radke. "I can almost hear that great laugh of hers."

"It can be kind of embarrassing in public," Emily admitted. Yet she was glad her mother's real laugh was back, could still remember how good it had felt to hear it again that day they'd peeked through the windows of the house with the widow's walk. "It sort of explodes right out of her face, you know what I mean?"

Dr. Radke chuckled. "That's why I like it; there's nothing fake about it."

Placing the photo of her mother on the top of the pile, Emily said, "I still can't believe she's the one who bought Sandy for me."

"Why's that?" asked the doctor.

"'Cause she doesn't love dogs like me and my dad do. He'll stop and talk to people he doesn't even know if they have a dog with them. He can't walk by one without patting it and saying hello, or telling me what the dog's thinking. But my mom's not like that, 'cause her family never had dogs when she was growing up. She says they're nothing but GI tracts with fur."

Dr. Radke jerked her head to the side, and the sip of coffee she'd just taken sprayed right out of her mouth.

Emily, who'd instinctively covered the pictures with her hands to protect them, asked, "Too hot?"

"Sorry," said Dr. Radke, who was now dabbing at the coffee spray on her desk with a tissue. "I never heard that one before."

"Oh, that's nothing," said Emily, quickly shoving her photos back into the envelope to ensure their safety. "You should hear what she says when she gets dog hair on her clothes."

"I don't think I want to know," said the doctor, whose face was still red and whose eyes were watery. "Excuse me while I blow my nose and collect what's left of my dignity."

"Sure," said Emily, placing the envelope in her backpack. Next time I bring pictures, she told herself, I'd better bring them in my album.

It didn't take Dr. Radke long to collect herself or her thoughts. "So—that your mom was the one who bought Sandy for you made it even more special, didn't it?" she calmly asked a minute later.

"Yeah," said Emily. "She loves me a lot."

"Well, now that you've caught me up on Sandy," said Dr. Radke, "how are you doing?"

Home Wrecker hasn't sold our house yet, so "I'm doing good." The truth was Emily was glad she didn't have to see Ms. Becker or the people who came to look at their house anymore. That she no longer had to scheme and lie was a relief, and it made the possibility of ever moving easier to forget.

"I missed seeing you last week," said Dr. Radke.

"Did my mom tell you why I didn't come?"

"Yes, and I think it was important that your family spent the day together."

On the anniversary of her brother's death, Emily's mother hadn't gone to work, Emily hadn't gone to school, and her father hadn't gone to the Palace. "We didn't plan it," said Emily, "it just sort of happened. My mom was on vacation, and I really didn't want to go to school, so she said I didn't have to. And 'cause we were both home, my dad decided to take the day off, too."

"Sometimes things work out better when you don't plan them," said the doctor.

Emily nodded. They hadn't planned on going to Denny's until her dad had said, "We don't have any eggs; let's go out for breakfast." Then, while they were eating there, her mom had said, "We should stop by Broadway Gardens and buy a new arrangement for the cemetery." And after they visited Jon's grave out at Calvary, they'd ended up stopping by that house for sale on the ocean, because her father hadn't seen it yet and it was right on their way home. It'd been like one of her dad's adventures, when they'd just get in the car and go.

"Would you like to talk about it?" Dr. Radke gently asked.

Emily looked down at her hands, unsure of what to say, or where to start. "Doesn't seem like it's been a whole year, you know?"

That thought was something that hadn't left Emily alone last Monday. It had woken her up that morning and followed her around all day, making her remember and compare every little thing. Before her alarm clock had even gone off, she'd been thinking how last year at that same time she and Jon were already downstairs with their swim bags packed, eating frosted cornflakes. She remembered how nervous she'd been because she was going to be in the same heat as Tracy Goodine in the freestyle, and how Jon, who was never afraid of his competition, had told her, "Don't worry, you'll smoke her. Just don't take a breath until two strokes out of your flip turn." Her brother, sitting across the table from her and making funny faces so she'd forget Tracy Goodine, so she'd laugh when he told her, "The best thing about having swim meets on Sunday is we don't have to go to church." That's how the day had gone, remembering things like that and asking her parents over and over what time it was so she could think about what they'd been doing right then the year before, when her brother was still alive: right now the swim meet was just starting; about now I was eating lunch at the food table with Cindy; right now I was changing in the locker room.

"Even though it was Monday instead of Sunday, and it was nice out instead of snowing, it seemed like it just happened," said Emily, for all the "what if"s and "if only"s had come back to her while she was standing in that cemetery staring at her brother's name. If only they'd canceled the swim meet because of the weather. If only. If only.

"The first anniversary is so difficult," said Dr. Radke.

"Even worse than Christmas," Emily agreed. "I kept thinking about him all day."

She'd kept remembering them fighting over who was going to get the front seat on the way home, the two of them slipping and sliding through the parking lot, Jon making it to the car first. Jon always won. Their father yelling at them, "Just get in!" Her, sulking in the back seat, so mad at being there that her last words to her brother when he was alive had been, "I hate you."

"Like living it all over again?" asked Dr. Radke.

Emily looked up at the doctor. "And wishing you could change it, even though you can't."

"Exactly. And I won't lie to you, Emily, it doesn't get any easier, just a little less painful. That's why I was glad your mom let you stay home from school. Families really need to be together on tough days like that."

"We watched videos of me and Jon when we were little," Emily told her. "We haven't done that in forever." She, Sandy, her mom and dad, all cuddled up on the bed watching Jon on her parents' TV, watching Christmas, birthdays, them playing with Sagey in the snow. Her brother the daredevil always jumping on or off or out of something, thinking he could fly. Always clowning for the camera and demanding attention: "Watch me! Watch me!"

"It was wicked funny," said Emily. "When I was a baby, he liked to hug me so tight my mom had to keep telling him, 'Be easy,' 'cause he was suffocating me. And in one video, he asked her, 'Can't we take her back to the hosbital and get a brother?' "

Emily started giggling. "You should see the one of us playing circus when I was about three. Sagey and I were the lions and Jon was the trainer guy, and every time he hit the floor with my dad's belt, we'd hop off one cushion and onto another."

Dr. Radke smiled at her. "That was a nice way to remember him, watching videos."

Yeah, thought Emily, because for a few hours last Monday she'd been allowed to travel back to the time when her house was white instead of pale yellow, when her father's hair was black instead of gray, when her mom could still pick her up and carry her around, and when Sagey wasn't too lame to run after a Frisbee. Her big brother, little, but alive again on her parents' TV, pulling her in his wagon, pushing her on the swing, feeding her Oreo cookies when she wasn't even six months old. "It was like we were a family again," said Emily, with a sad smile. "We were laughing so hard we were crying."

sixteen

"LOOK, IT'S STILL LIGHT out," said Janey as she and Emily left Dr. Radke's office. "Isn't it great?"

Looking over at the dirty snowbanks that were now only a few feet high, Emily said, "Spring's coming."

"When you live in Maine, it's called mud season, Em," Janey told her. "And with that little dog of yours, I'll be moppin' that kitchen floor twenty times a day. But I'll tell ya, I'm so sick of winter, I think we should do a drive-through at Dairy Queen to celebrate that it's almost over."

"But you gave up hot-fudge sundaes for Lent," Emily reminded her as Janey unlocked the car door.

"I didn't promise Jesus nothin' 'bout ice-cream cones. We've gotta move it, though; it's beano night."

Sliding into the front seat a moment later, Janey asked, "So how'd it go with Doc?"

"Good," Emily told her, as she strapped herself into her seatbelt. "She really liked the pictures of Sandy."

"Is that what you two were laughing about? I could hear you all the way out in the waiting room."

"Remember that time Jon made you laugh in McDonald's and your orange soda came out your nose? It was sorta like that."

"China Doll, the things you remember," said Janey, shaking her head. She started up the car. "Well, while you and Doc were hee-hawing in there, I was bustin' a gut myself. You know that lady I'd love to throttle? The one with the bleached hair who'd complain if it was rainin' dollar bills?"

"The skinny girl's mother?"

"That'd be the one, and she was makin' her usual nitpickin' noise. Yappin' that poor kid's ear off." Janey put the car in reverse and her story on hold while she backed out of the parking space.

"So?" asked Emily, who couldn't stand that woman, either, but who'd always been curious about her daughter. What was her problem? Why was she there? Although the adults in the waiting room sometimes chatted with one another, the kids never did. It wasn't a rule or anything; that's just the way it was. Still, even though they'd never exchanged one word, Emily had always felt a connection with that skinny girl. Every time they crossed paths in the waiting room, it was like seeing a stranger in a crowd that for a second you're sure you know. She might not know why the girl was there, or what her problem was, but one thing Emily was certain of: that girl had lost something as important as a brother.

"So there I was, pretendin' to be readin' *Teen People* and tryin' not to blow a gasket like I did that other time."

"You mean when you told her to put a plug in it 'cause she was giving you a headache right between the eyes?" asked Emily.

"Yeah, and I was almost to that point again today, when all of a sudden that little girl of hers—who never says a peep, just sits there like a deer caught in headlights—tells her, 'They're my nails, and I'll chew them if I want to.' Let me tell ya, I had to do some chewin' of my own so I didn't burst out laughin'. Bit my cheek so hard it still hurts. 'Bout time she stuck up for herself; it's been killin' me since September."

"Probably been killing her longer," said Emily.

"After, I told her mother, 'Good to see your daughter's makin' progress.' Told her, 'Dr. Radke's the best.' That's the only thing that woman and I agree on."

Emily looked out the window, thinking, Next week I'll say hi to that girl. Maybe even tell her my name.

"You're going to have to move to heaven or live with a lawyer who doesn't like kids," said Emily, crossing the cellar floor and trying her best to keep a straight face. "Home Wrecker sold our house."

April Fools!

"Shoot!" said Emily. She'd thought for sure she'd get him.

You're dealing with the jokemaster, he reminded her. *Got to do better than that.*

"I put Mom's alarm clock ahead an hour, so when she wakes up she'll think we missed church and I won't have to go."

Now you're talking, little sister, even though you stole that idea from me.

Emily started laughing, because she had, only the year Jon had done it, he'd turned all the clocks, even their parents' watches, back an hour instead of ahead. Their mother had arrived at the hospital for her seven-thirty case at ten past six, and their dad, who was supposed to give a talk at the University of Southern Maine, found the lecture hall empty, so he'd left, thinking he had the wrong day. "What else can I do? I got to make up for last year." There hadn't been any jokes or anything funny then. That was the day they'd taken skin from her bottom and put it on her ankle.

Hide the coffee before Dad gets up. He'll run right down to Dunkin' Donuts if he thinks we're out of it, and you can go with him and get a chocolate-glazed cruller.

Emily giggled.

And here's one for Janey. . . .

That afternoon, when Emily went down-cellar to work on her solo, she told Jon, "You're still the King. I got everybody. You should have seen Dad, he trashed the kitchen big-time looking for those two cans of coffee I hid. He looked just like that guy in the smoking commercial who can't find a cigarette. That was da bomb."

Da bomb?

"That's what all the kids say now instead of 'awesome.'" Emily sat down on the exercise mat, and Sandy immediately pounced on her. Laughing, Emily pushed the dog's wet nose away from her. "Go play with the puppy," she ordered. "I have to practice."

Sandy took off for the mirror and Emily began to stretch out. She'd been working hard all week, for now she had a reason to—she'd found the music for her solo.

After searching for something new and coming up empty, she'd resigned herself to doing the solo she'd prepared the year before, but as Janey liked to say, "If you stop looking for something, that's when you find it."

And that's just how it had happened. She and Janey had been sitting in the parking lot at Dairy Queen, working on their soft-serve cones that Emily had ordered all by herself, when a song started playing on the radio. There was no piano, no guitar, no one singing backup, just a lone voice, and as she'd listened to that soulful sound coming through the speakers, she knew right then that it would be the music she would dance to.

When the song was over, Janey had told her, "They played that at Jon's funeral."

"I know," Emily had answered, even though she hadn't.

As soon as they'd gotten home, Emily had found the song on the Internet and downloaded Faith Hill's rendition of it onto a CD. Although the deadline for solo selections had already gone by three weeks before, she was certain it wouldn't take her long to choreograph a dance to the music that had moved her and Janey to tears in the Dairy Queen parking lot. She also figured if she had it almost finished by the following week Debbie would let her switch for sure. After all, some of the girls had barely begun working on theirs; how could Debbie say no?

Now, as she completed her barre exercises, Emily was eager to practice. She wiped the sweat from her forehead and went to track down Sandy, who'd finally become bored with the mirror game.

Earlier that week, Emily had moved all the furniture to give herself a bigger stage, and now she had to squirm her way around that furniture in order to get Sandy. The dog was under the pool table, sniffing—searching, Emily assumed—either for Jon or for one of her balls. "Come on, Silly Sandy. Time for you to be the audience." She picked up the puppy, who was getting heavier and harder for her to carry, and brought her over to the couch. "Now, you stay right here, or I'll have to put you in your house upstairs," Emily warned. "Understand?"

The dog opened its mouth and yawned at her, then crawled to the edge of the couch, looking for the safest place to jump off. Emily was about to scold her when Sandy suddenly rolled over on her back. She lay there with her head tilted backward and her skinny tail thumping, just as if someone were rubbing her belly.

Go ahead; she'll stay.

"Thanks," said Emily, catching a slight whiff of hair gel and a sudden chill that prickled the hair on her forearms. "Look," she told him, holding out her arm. "It's like touching that static ball at the science museum."

Today, please.

"I'm going, I'm going," Emily told him. She pushed the power button on the stereo and, armed with the remote, walked to the center of her makeshift stage, her mind now focused on the sequence of steps she'd already learned. The first night she'd danced to the song it'd been easy, she'd just let her body go with no thought about what she was doing, allowed the music and emotion to just take her. She'd gone to bed that night with her earphones on, replaying "Amazing Grace" over and over in the dark, memorizing the voice and the words, which later followed her into her dreams. But the freedom and pleasure of that first night had disappeared once she'd begun the real work the following afternoon, the work of breaking the music down into sections and trying to make her body memorize by rote the sequence of dance steps she'd instinctively created.

To her, choreographing a song was like writing a story. It had a beginning, a middle, and an end, each section of the music telling her something different, just like a scene within a story. It was a way of thinking that came naturally to her, and, applying the same tools her father had taught her for writing, she created her own interpretation, using arabesques, pirouettes, and jumps instead of words. She used arm movements and poses like adjectives; chassés and triplet runs as adverbs; facial expressions and body language to capture the emotion of the character; balancés and pas de bourrées to link dance steps together like sentences in a paragraph.

So where are we?

Emily hesitated, trying to remember where she'd left off the day before. "We stopped right after she sings 'the hour I first believed' and I relevé with my arms reaching up like this. Remember?"

Yeah, I liked that part.

Emily smiled, pleased. Jon had never cared about her dancing when he was alive. She figured the only reason he'd gone to her recitals was to watch the older girls in their leotards. "I'll practice up to that point a few times," she told him. "Then we can start on the new stuff."

But a few times ended up turning into thirteen, because she kept making mistakes. After the last go-through, she was so winded and frustrated she snapped off the remote and threw it across the room. "That friggin' 'once was lost' part is driving me crazy!"

I noticed.

"And this stupid ankle. I hate it! Keeps making me screw up that jump." She sat down and peeled off her sweaty ballet slipper, then the elastic ankle brace she had to wear. "Look at it; it's three times the size of my other one." And that wasn't too much of an exaggeration; even her toes were swollen. Leaning forward, she began to massage her foot, the knot in her arch hard as rock. Spotting blood on her fingers, she inspected her foot closer; it was coming from her plantar warts. She'd picked away too much skin the day before after using the Compound W, and now the warts between her toes were so raw they were beading up blood. It's not fair, she thought, glaring down at the ugly scars on her leg, at that ankle the size of a grapefruit, at those disgusting, bleeding warts.

After all the mistakes and her inability to nail that jump, it was just too much. She burst into tears, the anger and frustration coming out of her in sobs. She was crying so hard her whole body was shaking, though some of that could have been from the room's temperature, which had suddenly grown so cold she could see the heat rising off her sweaty body. And just then, out of the corner of her eye, Emily caught sight of Sandy's favorite ball rolling across the floor. She glanced over at the couch, but the dog was sound asleep. "H-how'd you do that?" she hiccupped, through her tears.

April Fools!

"Sweet. That's the kind of stuff you should do when Home Wrecker's showing people around down here." She removed the sweatband from her head and used it to wipe her face. "You could float a pool stick through the air or something."

I'm not here to scare people; I'm just here because of you.

Emily stared down at the ball that was no longer moving and felt guilty. If it weren't for her, he'd probably be up in heaven right now, swimming through the clouds, or hanging out with Grampa, or playing Frisbee with Sagey—doing something a lot better than listening and watching her bawl over her stupid warts.

She pulled her brace and her clammy ballet slipper back on. "Okay," she said, getting to her feet. "Let's take it from the top."

seventeen

EMILY'S PLAN was a simple one. She'd take so long putting on her sweats and sneakers after dance class that she'd be the last girl there. That's when she'd ask Debbie about switching. Emily was certain the teacher would say it was okay once she heard the music. The only problem Emily anticipated was the length of the song. The spring recital included all of Debbie's classes, which consisted of five different levels and ranged from four-year-olds to girls in high school. Levels one through three each performed two dances; levels four and five performed three, plus duets and solos. Because of the time required for that many dances, duets and solos were strictly limited to two minutes. Emily's song was three minutes and forty-one seconds long.

I'll just tell her what Dad says, thought Emily, as she walked up the stairs to the dance studio—a book's as long as it has to be. Only instead of "book," she'd say "dance."

During class, Emily kept thinking about the CD in her ballet bag. She was so excited about having Debbie hear the song that she was having trouble concentrating. Even while her body was going through the motions of her parts in *The Four Seasons*, her mind was on the other dance she'd been practicing in her cellar. Although none of the other girls seemed to notice, her instructor did.

"Emily, stay with us," Debbie told her. "You're a full beat off."

"Sorry," Emily apologized, her face turning crimson. She was one of the students Debbie never had to talk to, who always came to class prepared and focused. Pay attention, she told herself, pay attention.

And for the next forty-five minutes, that seemed to work. But just before class was supposed to end, while she was waiting at the back of the line for her turn to pas-de-chat across the studio floor, Emily's attention drifted again. Closing her eyes, she let herself hear the music inside her head: "A-maz-ing Grace! H-ow sweet the sound. . . ." The words and the beautiful range of that voice flowed through her like a current, provoking emotions she couldn't control. She became so lost in the song that, when the girl behind her gave her a nudge, that was what Emily automatically danced to across the studio floor.

"Where did that come from?" asked Debbie with a confused look on her face.

Emily heard a rush of whispers from the group of girls who'd gone before her. Mortified, she looked behind her as if searching for an explanation, but all she found was the last girl in line still standing there. Staring back at Debbie, who was waiting for an answer, Emily admitted, "I forgot what I was doing."

A round of giggles, another rustle of whispered words behind hands, and then her teacher's voice, gentle but stern: "Get back in line, Emily. And this time, please try to remember what we're doing."

Although Emily had made a fool out of herself, she was more ashamed about wasting her teacher's time. "I'm sorry."

Debbie accepted her apology with a nod and told her, "See me after class."

Which was something Emily had planned to do, but not this way, not because she hadn't paid attention. And a few minutes later, while the other girls exchanged their ballet shoes for sneakers, grabbed their coats, and hurried from the studio, she sat there thinking: You've really done it now, Ollie.

Becky, her favorite friend in class, leaned over and whispered in her ear. "I thought it was great. Want me to wait for you?"

"No," said Emily as she put her sweatpants on. "But thanks for asking."

"See you Thursday, then," Becky told her and gave her a comforting pat on the back.

Emily waited nervously as a couple of the "kiss-up" mothers—who always had to talk and brag to Debbie after class—held her teacher hostage by the door. She was glad her mother never embarrassed her like that and always waited in the car, like Emily asked her to. She was also glad she had parents who let her think for herself—she wasn't even going to tell them she was switching songs; she wanted her solo to be a surprise. But if Mom were like them, Emily now thought, looking over at the two still hounding Debbie by the door, I'd never be able to do something like that. As Tammy, who also made her mother wait in the car, liked to say, "Those girls can't sneeze without their mothers there to wipe their noses."

"Sorry to keep you waiting, Emily," said Debbie once she was finally free of them.

Emily felt her breath catch as she watched her teacher—who had long legs and the slender build and carriage of a dancer—move across the empty studio, chiffon skirt lifting like a sigh in the wake of her grace. Sometimes Debbie's beauty startled her, made her wonder why she'd given up a career as a professional ballerina to have a family and teach. "That's okay," she said.

"I was a little concerned about you," said Debbie, now so close that Emily could smell her juniper perfume. "You weren't your usual studious self tonight. I just wanted to make sure you were all right."

Emily felt her teacher's hand rest lightly upon her shoulder. "I'm really sorry about class," Emily told her. "I needed to talk to you about something and I couldn't stop thinking about it."

"It must be important, then," said Debbie.

"It is." Emily opened up her ballet bag and took out the CD. "I want to switch the music for my solo. I don't want to do 'Greensleeves' anymore."

Debbie raised her eyebrows. "It's a little late for that. Selections were a month ago; rehearsals start next week."

"I know, that's why I've been working every day since I heard this." Emily held up the CD that she'd made of the song she downloaded off the Internet, an act of piracy she'd learned from Jon.

"Do you have time for us to listen to it?" asked Debbie.

"Oh, sure," Emily told her, her spirits lifting. "My mother doesn't mind waiting in the parking lot. She says sitting in the car's the only time she gets to be alone all day."

"Which song?" asked Debbie.

Smiling, Emily handed the CD to her teacher as if she were giving Debbie a gift. "There's only one on it," she said, feeling a tingle of excitement that made her promise, "You're going to love it."

But Emily was wrong, and she knew that even before the song was over just by the look on her teacher's face.

"It's a lovely song," said Debbie, clicking off the CD player the second it was over. "But it has words. I don't allow that."

To Emily her teacher's response felt like a punch in the stomach—all that work, all that time. "Why?"

"This is classical ballet," Debbie explained. "Instrumental music only."

"But her voice *is* an instrument," Emily argued, her face warming with anger. "And the words are the music."

Debbie took a step backward as though she, too, had just been punched. "You really feel strongly about this."

Standing there with her hands on her hips and blinking back tears, Emily nodded. No one was going to take this song away from her—enough had been taken already. That shy girl who would have given in didn't live there any longer. "I won't dance to anything else."

Debbie began massaging her temples like she had a serious headache. "Ballet to vocals? Madame Baudelaire would be spinning in her grave." She sighed and looked down at Emily. "How much have you done?"

Emily kicked off her sneakers in about three seconds and ripped off her sweatpants almost faster. "I'll show you."

At the first sound of the long A in "Amazing," Emily glided forward in a diagonal direction, her feet carrying her through the delicate steps she'd practiced so well, her arms, shoulders, neck gracefully capturing the rhythm of the music and the story of the words.

"Lovely arms," said Debbie. "Very nice, very nice."

But Emily was already too focused on the song to hear her, its tempo building and her body responding, her turns quick, sharp, and fitting the beat of the music exactly. Posture firm, eyes spotting the open doorway with each turn, she moved across the spacious studio, finally free to make the steps as large as they should be. And then she was there, in that dreamlike place where time seemed to stand still, where the world fell away till only the song existed—dancing, dancing—her arms and footwork in perfect harmony with the music, her body telling the story. Dancing. Dancing. The adrenaline surging as she soared airborne into a grand jeté.

"Are you okay?" asked Debbie, kneeling on the floor, her knowledgeable hands already checking her student for damage.

Emily, whose ankle had buckled on the landing, had fallen so fast and hard it'd dazed her. Still stunned, but aware enough to know that the song and her chance were slipping away from her, she pushed herself up off the floor. Although her knee was on fire with a floor-burn she'd gotten right through her tights, she panted, "Let me try it again."

"We're going to have to change that jump," said Debbie, whose probing fingers were now pressing against Emily's throbbing ankle. "It's the right idea, but this foot's not strong enough for anything that ambitious—that's why your ankle rolled when you landed."

Looking down at the top of her teacher's head and the tightly plaited bun, Emily wondered, Change the jump?

"And I don't think this is giving you enough support," said Debbie, worming a finger beneath the elastic brace. "You need to start taping this ankle before you practice; that will help. Before class on Thursday, I'll show you how to do it. Till then, you rest it; no working out."

"So I can do it?"

Debbie rose to her feet with the fluid agility of someone much younger. "It'll open up a whole can of worms for me," she said, gliding over to the CD player to shut off Faith Hill, who was now almost finished singing the last verse. "You'll be setting a new precedent. And to be honest, it's against my better judgment."

Emily exhaled, already anticipating the "but" that was coming.

"But it's obvious to me how much time you've put into this piece, and what it means to you. You know, my level-five students are more technically advanced, but when it comes to creativity and projecting emotion, you're way ahead of them. And believe me, Emily, that is the *hardest* thing to teach." Debbie returned the disc to its case. "After everything you've been through, I don't think it'd be fair for me to say no, do you?"

"That's exactly how I feel," Emily agreed, taking the CD from her.

"Besides," said Debbie, pointing toward the barre and the mirror that ran along the wall behind it, "sometimes that teacher has to remember this is Maine and not New York; has to remind herself of the chances of ever having one of her students make it that far."

For a moment, they both stared at the reflection across the room, Emily suddenly acutely aware of how puny she looked standing beside Debbie's tall, willowy figure; how crooked her posture was compared to her teacher's, her left hip jutting out at an odd angle, her whole body shifted to the right, as if she were leaning on a cane. Baryshnikov and Tiny Tim, she thought. The truth in the mirror brought back that same numbing sensation she'd felt the first time she'd seen the hardware sticking out of her leg; the same roaring in her ears when her eyes didn't want to believe what they were seeing. She quickly turned away from the mirror.

So did Debbie. "Of course we'll have to cut it down, but we'll work on that together."

Emily stared at the floor feeling humiliated by what she'd just seen.

"And I think it'd be best if you didn't tell the other girls about this. They'll all want to change their songs, and it's too late in the year for us to do that."

Emily couldn't look at her teacher. She needed to get out of there.

"So, when we start solo rehearsals after class, I'll always have you go last. Okay?"

Falling back on anger to save what was left of her dignity,

Emily told her teacher, "That's fine. I don't want anyone to copy me anyway."

Emily limped across the empty parking lot, every muscle in her body aching. In the hazy glow of the headlights she could see the cool drizzle that felt so good against her face. When she opened the car door, the heat and her mother's voice seemed to hit her at the same time. "I was getting worried; I was just about to go inside to look for you."

In the dim dome light, her mother looked washed out. "Sorry," Emily told her. "Debbie asked me to stay after so she could help me with my solo." She threw her stuff on the floor and climbed in.

"No coat, no sweatpants," her mother sighed. "You know better than that, Em."

Emily buckled her seatbelt and rolled the window down to get some air. The car was boiling.

"You're going to catch a cold."

Who cares, thought Emily. "No, I won't," she said, "I'm sweating."

"Until you have an M.D. after your name, you just listen to your mother."

"I'm not going to be a doctor," snapped Emily. Or a dancer, either, she thought, and suddenly the devastation she'd felt back in the studio caught up with her. "That was Jon, your favorite. Remember?"

"I think that's enough, Emily."

But it wasn't. Leaning forward, Emily reached for the radio to find a song her mother couldn't stand, and it was only then that she realized she was sitting in the front seat. For a second she hesitated, then she changed the station.

"Turn that back," her mother scolded. "I don't want to listen to that rap-crap in my car."

Which was exactly why Emily now gave the volume knob a healthy twist.

"What's this all about?" her mother asked, and as she brushed Emily's hand away from the dashboard, the touch of her daughter's wrist stopped her. "You're sitting in the front seat?"

"Let's just go," Emily told her. "I need to ice my stupid ankle."

Her mother clicked off the radio. "We're not going anywhere until you tell me what's the matter."

Emily glanced toward the building. Debbie was probably going to walk out the door any second and see them still sitting there. "Can't we just go, Mom? Please?"

Her mother sighed, put the car in gear, and drove off.

Emily shimmied closer to the door and with her face to the open window stared blankly at the rainbow halos around the passing streetlights. The comment about her brother and the brief radio battle had used up all the fight she had left. She closed her eyes, tried to hold back the tears that were burning behind her lids. Her solo had been perfect up to that point. Perfect. But she'd seen something in the studio mirror that had scared her worse than that fall, something that had shattered a dream she'd had since she was four years old. She was never going to be Debbie; never going to be the student who made it that far.

"Did Debbie say something about your solo?" her mother asked with concern.

What could she have said? thought Emily. Stop wasting your parents' money 'cause your dream's never going to happen?

"Well?" pressed her mom.

The worry in her mother's voice made Emily turn away from the window. She stared across the seat at her mother, whom a moment ago she'd wanted to hurt because she'd been hurt, and gave her the only "sorry" she could. "She said I'm more creative than her level-five students." Now leave me alone.

"Good for you, Em," her mother said enthusiastically. "That's a great compliment. That must have made you feel good."

"Yeah." But it was what her teacher *hadn't* said while they were comparing themselves in the mirror that had had the most impact. Any other time Debbie would have corrected her posture, would have scolded her into standing up straight, and all the experience people-watching with her dad had allowed Emily to understand why her teacher didn't. She'd seen that flash of pity, had pegged the look in Debbie's eyes with no trouble at all: She's never going to make it with that ankle.

One glance in a mirror at the right moment and Emily had seen her limitations. You couldn't make a Baryshnikov out of a Tiny Tim. One look, barely longer than a heartbeat, and she'd had to face something she'd known for months but hadn't wanted to admit: she was never going to dance the parts of Odette and Odile on that magical stage in New York City. She was going to have to be something else, and the thought of that made her feel like she'd just lost Jon all over again.

eighteen

WARMER DAYS and April rain melted the last traces of dirty snow. Mud season came, and the Becker and Brook Realtors sign was recovered from its wintry grave, washed off, and returned to its S-hooks at the end of Emily's driveway.

Over the course of those days and weeks, when the rock-hard ground became soft again, when daylight lengthened and robins returned, Emily and Sandy spent a lot more time outside. Emily no longer had to keep Sandy on a leash, for the dog stuck to her like a shadow. Together they'd explore the wetland down by the culvert where cattails grew along the banks, and hunt for tadpoles in the shallow, muddy water like she and Jon used to do when they were little.

And often, while they were roaming the three-acre property where Emily grew up, she'd tell the dog stories about things that had happened. "See that tree? One spring a raccoon family lived in it," she'd begin, and then she'd tell Sandy all about it: how there had been two babies and a mother; how they'd peek their heads out of the hollow circle a good twenty feet above the ground; how once, while her family was having a barbecue, all three came out on the branch to watch her, Jon, and their cousins play kickball; and how her aunt May had pitched a fit about them getting rabies.

No matter where or what they were doing, there always seemed to be a story for Emily to tell, her recollection of details sometimes as pretty and colorful as the crocuses she'd collect for Sagey's grave; sometimes a story so funny she'd laugh out loud; and once in a while, one so sad it'd make her cry when she told it. Sandy was a good audience and never seemed to mind that Emily had a habit of repeating those stories over and over, each time adding a few new details, some of them true, but most of them made up to add a little more danger or drama.

Perhaps it was the restlessness that comes with spring after a long cold winter, or maybe it was seeing that sign again at the end of her driveway, but there was an undercurrent of urgency during those afternoon adventures with her dog. It was as if she had to see and touch and remember everything, because her time there was running out. She was so sure of that feeling that she began collecting mementos to add to the treasure box beneath her bed where she stored all her important keepsakes, like Sagey's collar; one of her brother's swimming medals, which she'd taken from her mother's drawer; a Kennedy half-dollar that Esther had given her; newspaper clippings—Jon's obituary; the first picture of her house in the Realtors section of the *Maine Sunday Telegram.*

She selected things from her yard that had meaning: the

velvety top of a cattail, a withered chestnut from the Raccoon Tree, a pencil sketch she'd hastily drawn of Sagey's grave, a chip of red paint from the swing set, a rusty spoon she'd found in the sumac bushes where she and Jon and Nate used to build forts. They were things she could hold and look at, things that would keep her from forgetting those stories when she no longer lived there. As she put it to Dr. Radke during one of their sessions, "Sometimes I feel like Dorothy in *The Wizard of Oz*. You know, when the Wicked Witch of the West turns over that hourglass? It's like there's no way I can stop the sand."

The first Sunday in May, it was so nice out that, while they were driving over to the house on the ocean to finally see what it looked like on the inside, Emily's mother said, "It's warm enough to thaw the ice out of my bones."

"She stole that line from Janey," Emily told her father.

But her dad wasn't listening to them. "If I'd known Jack was the one handling this place I would have called a long time ago. I haven't seen him in I don't know how long—twenty years?"

"Have I ever met him?" asked Emily's mother.

"I don't think so. We grew up together on the Hill. Now he lives down in Kennebunk, but I think his mother still lives in Portland. Remember that story I wrote about the kid playing baseball? That was him. Boy, could he park it. And *fast*—when he'd steal a base, all you'd see is dust. After high school he played in the minors for a couple of years down in Florida, but a month after he started playing for the Padres he blew out his knee stealing third base. Can't picture him selling real estate."

Ten minutes later, the first thing her dad said when he shook hands with this man, who was dressed in jeans, tee shirt, and a baseball cap, was, "Great to see you, Jack. God, you haven't changed a bit. Look the same as you did in high school."

"And you're just as ugly, too," Jack answered.

While the adults were laughing about that, Emily was wondering—were they really the same age? Her father looked so much older.

"I'm sorry about the clothes," Jack told Emily's mother. "I usually dress a little better than this, but my son has a game at one and I'm the coach."

"It's Theresa," said Emily's mom, extending her hand. "And we should be the ones apologizing for taking you away from your family on a Sunday."

"Jack Flaherty. It's nice to meet you. And don't feel guilty. Mikey and I go a long way back—I owe him more than a few favors." And then, nodding at Emily, he told her dad, "She looks like May."

I'm a lot prettier than Aunt May, thought Emily, thank you very much.

"But even prettier," Jack added.

"That's just what I was thinking," Emily told him honestly, and once again all the adults laughed.

"This is our daughter, Emily," said her father. "She *used* to be shy."

Once the introductions were over and her father and his friend started catching up on people from the old neighborhood, Emily stopped listening. Whenever her dad ran into anyone who called him Mikey, he'd gab for an hour.

Her mother knew it, too. Leaning toward her daughter, she whispered, "Let's take a walk around to the front."

"Can Sandy come?" Emily asked, looking back at the car, and the dog, whose head was sticking out the window. "She's never seen the ocean yet."

Her mother hedged for a second. "She'll have to stay on a leash."

She doesn't need it, thought Emily, but, just to make her mother happy, she did what she was told.

This time it was a lot different: the yard no longer white; the journey to the front of the house so much easier without the snow.

"Look," said her mother, pointing at the wild rosebushes growing along the side of the porch. "I didn't notice those before."

Neither had Emily. "I bet they'll be the pink kind they have at Two Lights and Crescent Beach," she told her mother. "The ones that smell wicked nice."

They walked across the ragged grass, still brown in places, the scent of decay, seaweed, and ocean all mixed together. Sandy kept tugging on her leash, excited by the new territory and new smells, and because it was one of Sandy's favorite things to do, Emily warned her, "Don't roll in anything dead."

Still, she let the dog pull her through the yard, which didn't look as large as it had last winter beneath that blanket of snow. Even the stairs leading to the beach below seemed closer, and not as rickety or scary as she'd remembered.

A few minutes later, her dad and his friend joined them. Bending down to pat Sandy, who was wagging her tail like she already trusted him, Jack told her parents, "The property taxes are going to kill you, and it needs a lot of work—new roof, wiring, furnace, updated kitchen, cosmetics throughout. But it's hard finding land like this anymore, and no one will ever be able to build in front of you and ruin that view."

"It's beautiful," said her mother as they all looked out at the ocean, the sky on this day blue instead of gray, with sunlight shimmering off the water like tinsel.

"Peaceful?" asked her dad—as though it was a word he wasn't sure of.

"I'll give you a heads-up about the inside, though," Jack told them. "It's not too shiny, and it's going to need a lot of love. That's why I didn't even bother to push it this winter; I knew it wouldn't show as well." Then, addressing Emily's mother, he said, "From what Mikey tells me, you've already seen a few places, so you know what's out there, and what you're looking for. Like I told him, that's half the battle—knowing what you want."

Unlike Ms. Becker, who would have given them a detailed tour, pointing out all the good points and possibilities, Jack just handed her dad the key and told him, "Take all the time you want. You can drop this off at the office tomorrow and tell me what you think. If you're interested enough, we'll come back here and go through it again together."

"Sounds good," her dad said, shaking his friend's hand. "And thanks again, Jack, for letting us see it on the spur of the moment."

"*Really*," her mother agreed. "We've had our eye on it for a while but haven't had the time to check into it."

"No problem," said Jack. "Things have a way of happening. Today's paper was the first time I've run the ad since last fall." Glancing down at his watch, he added, sincerely, "Wish I didn't have to split on you."

"Please, don't let us hold you up," her mother told him. "I'd feel terrible if you were late for your son's game."

"So would I," said her dad.

"I'll catch you tomorrow, then," said Jack, still looking at them, but already walking backward.

"Good luck with the game," her dad called.

Jack waved at them. "Thanks! Enjoy the day!"

"What a nice man," said her mother, after he was gone.

Her father nodded. "He really felt bad when I told him about Jon. Said it'd kill him."

"Did you tell him it does?" asked her mother.

"Didn't have to. Told him, 'You do what you have to do to get by.'"

The sound of resolve in her father's voice seemed almost as strange as hearing Jon's name spoken out in the open, outside, where anyone could hear. It made Emily's throat tighten, made it hard for her to swallow.

"Are you ready for this?" her mother asked, staring up at the house, which needed paint, new screens, new steps.

"Just remember what he said," her father answered. "It's not too shiny on the inside."

And her father's friend, who'd grown up with him on the Hill, who'd once played baseball for the Padres, hadn't lied to them.

Emily's mother had dragged her through a number of houses since that cold, windy day they'd peeked into the windows of this one. The others had been new, bigger, full of pretty things and polished furniture, their huge kitchens and carpeted bedrooms right out of those magazines her mom had started to buy. So Emily felt a little weird as she and Sandy followed her parents through the empty rooms of this one, whose dark woodwork and faded wallpaper seemed ancient, whose rugless floors sighed and creaked beneath her father's heavy footsteps, whose kitchen was the color of an avocado and didn't even have a dishwasher. Yet it was the sense of neglect and the emptiness of the place that appealed to her, that made her think how lonely the windows looked without any curtains. And, unlike those pretty houses she'd been through that needed nothing, this was the first place that made her wonder where they'd put the Christmas tree and how her white canopy bed would look in one of its rooms.

Now, as her parents moved on to the attic, their echoing voices still discussing the kitchen that needed to be gutted, Emily remained where she was. Scrutinizing the bedroom that might be hers, whose plaster walls had cracks like veins, she tried to imagine what it would look like wallpapered with tiny yellow flowers, with white woodwork instead of brown. After contemplating where she'd put all her things and what she might have to give up in order to hang her clothes in that tiny closet, she printed her name in the dust on one of its windowsills.

"Come on, Em," her mother called from the attic's stairwell.

"I'm coming," Emily yelled back, but lingered by the window a moment longer, transfixed by the view and a question she couldn't answer.

Staring out at the rocks and the water and a blue sky that seemed to go on forever, she asked the dog, patiently waiting at her feet, "What do you think, Sandy? Waking up to this instead of the Raccoon Tree and the Muldoons' backyard?" And suddenly feeling guilty for even wondering, she quickly erased her name.

nineteen

ALTHOUGH SHE KNEW every note, step, and movement by heart, Emily couldn't shake the awful feeling that she was never going to be ready for the recital that was now only five days away. Looking back, she wasn't sure where the time had gone. It was sort of like the snow: one day it'd just disappeared, and, seemingly the next, all she'd needed was a jacket outside. Or sort of like those leaves she was staring at through Dr. Radke's window—once they'd been the colors of an Indian paintbrush, and now they were green.

"It's come so fast," she told Dr. Radke. "And I've got such a busy week: regular practice tomorrow, rehearsal at the high school Thursday, dress rehearsal Friday, the recital Saturday night, and there's something else I'm supposed to do."

"That *is* a busy week."

"Oh, yeah," said Emily, remembering what that something else was, "I have to go shopping with my dad sometime, 'cause

Mother's Day's on Sunday." Then, looking up at Dr. Radke, she asked, "You are coming, right?"

"I'm not sure if I can talk my boys into it, but I'll be there."

"If you want a good seat, you have to go early," Emily warned her. "My gram always gets there an hour before it starts."

Placing a hand over Emily's drumming fingers, Dr. Radke assured her, "I'll be there early."

"Thanks. And, sorry, I'm just wicked nervous. It's like a hundred times worse than a swim meet. Like part of me doesn't want Saturday to ever come, and the other part can't wait for it to be over."

Dr. Radke smiled at her. "Do you want to know a secret? Every time I have to give a speech at a convention, I feel the same way. I'm a nervous wreck."

"Know what Janey told me that might help you?" Emily asked the doctor.

"What's that?"

"If you picture everyone in the audience sitting there in their underwear, you won't be nervous. Works for me when I have to give book reports."

That night, when Emily went down-cellar to practice, the first thing she told Jon was, "As if I need one more thing to worry about: Mom can't pick up my costume."

Why?

"A liver resection, one of those Whipple things that take forever." Emily scooped up Sandy's ball and pegged it across the room, and the dog raced after it. "She said it'd be too late to drop by Gram's by the time she got done operating."

Ask Dad.

"No way I'm bugging him. He's so into that book he's writing now, he's still wearing the same clothes I saw him in on Friday."

I'm glad he's "In the Zone" again.

So was she. "Yeah, Janey only has to take the bottles back once a month now. Don't know what he's working on, but when he starts asking what day it is, you know it's something good. I would have had Janey take me on the way home from Dr. Radke's, but it's beano night."

Mom will get it tomorrow.

"Don't understand why someone who can suture bowels together and stitch people up can't sew a little chiffon on a leotard." Originally, Emily was just going to wear the costume she'd gotten for her solo the year before, because she'd never used it and no one had seen it. Although she'd loved that costume when she and her mom had bought it last year—the lavender color, the silver spangles, the puffy tutu that floated around her like a cloud—when she'd tried it on a week ago, she'd hated it, thought it looked like something only a little kid would want to wear. "But you know Mom, she'll throw away a shirt before she'll waste her time sewing a button back on."

Want some cheese with that whine? At least she was cool about you changing costumes at the last second.

Her brother was right. She'd expected their mother to have a meltdown when she'd told her, "It doesn't fit me anymore; I grew out of it," but all her mother had said was, "Shoot, that cost a fortune, and it looked so nice on you." And then her mother had rearranged her whole schedule so she could take Emily back down to the ballet store where even tights cost a fortune. But at that late date, they didn't have anything left that Emily liked, and to order a costume would take too long. It'd been the same story at the six other stores they'd gone to between Portland and Augusta, and when they'd left the last one empty-handed, her mother, who hated to shop, had told her, "Don't worry, Em; there's always Boston."

"I know," Emily now told her brother, as she began taping her ankle. "She was even going to take me all the way to Boston to find one." But Emily had thought of another idea during the drive back from Augusta—she'd just make one. After all, she knew what she wanted: something simple, something that would bring attention to her arms and not her footwork, something that flowed when she moved. By the time they'd reached Lewiston, the costume had materialized in her mind. She already owned a white leotard and white chiffon skirt and white tights. All she needed to do was attach a cape of chiffon to the arms of her leotard and she'd look just like the Russian ballerina who'd danced the part of Giselle. So, instead of going to Boston, they'd bought three yards of white chiffon at Jo-Ann Fabrics and then ate at Friendly's on the way home. "That's the funny thing about Mom," said Emily, putting her ankle brace over her taped foot. "Just when you think she's going to be mad at you most, she isn't."

Sandy came over and nuzzled her face into Emily's lap. "You're my swimmer-girl, aren't you, pal?" Rubbing her hands over the dog's silky ears, she told Jon, "Wish you could have seen her, she was wicked funny. A big wave knocked her over, and just like that"—she snapped her fingers—"she taught herself to swim. But she didn't like those seagulls, did you, girl?" Emily laughed at the memory of her dog stalking those birds that had taken off like airplanes whenever Sandy had come too close.

Tell me about the house again.

"I already told you everything yesterday." The only thing she hadn't told him was how much fun they'd had. Because her dad's friend had said, "Take all the time you want," after going through the house they'd spent over an hour down on the beach. While she and her dad had thrown driftwood sticks into the waves for Sandy to fetch and scouted for crabs in the rocky pools left behind by the tide, her mom, who was always moving, had napped on the sunny rocks like a sea lion.

Be a nice place for a dog to live.

"The best," said Emily; then she slowly glanced around the cellar, comparing it with the other one, which didn't have pine paneling, a tiled floor, a real ceiling, or a mirror with a ballet barre. "But that cellar doesn't even have windows," she told her brother. All it had was concrete walls, a big black sink, a furnace, and a nasty-looking hole in the floor where water drained out. "Only thing that'd want to live down there is mildew and spiders."

twenty

WHEN EMILY GOT home from rehearsal at the high-school auditorium on Thursday night, the first place she headed for was the cellar. Slamming the door behind her, she stomped down the stairs, wanting to break something. When she got to the bottom step, she settled for winging her ballet bag across the floor.

Just a guess—rehearsal didn't go well?

Ripping off her jacket, Emily told her brother, "Try awful, terrible, disastrous, the worst."

Glad someone was having a good time.

Emily ignored the comment; she wasn't in the mood for jokes. Tonight had been the first rehearsal of all five levels of Debbie's classes at the high school, and it'd gone badly. Although they'd been working on their dances since September, no one in her level-four class besides her seemed to know what they were doing. They kept messing up and making excuses—blaming it on the stage, which was bigger than they were used to; on Lindsey, who was home with the chicken pox, leaving Tammy without a partner; on being nervous; on all the noise the other classes were making. The third time Mindy messed up on their intro to *The Four Seasons,* Emily had wanted to yell at her for making them look like fools, and maybe would have if Debbie hadn't: "No more excuses! Now, focus, ladies, and do it right!"

And on top of that, she'd gotten a lousy placement in the program for her solo. Tammy's came early, between the two level-one dances, and Becky's didn't come until after the last of level five—they'd have plenty of time to get ready for theirs, but she'd be lucky if she had time to change costumes. But the real reason Emily was so angry, and why she now punched one of the couch pillows with a tight fist, was because: "They wouldn't even talk to me! Not even Becky, and she's supposed to be my best friend there!"

How come?

"'Cause of my solo." Until tonight, no one except Debbie had known she was dancing to "Amazing Grace." Like her parents, the kids in her class had just assumed she was still doing her dance from "Greensleeves." As soon as her music began, "vocals" was whispered like a dirty word, and had raced through the auditorium faster than fire in a stiff wind.

"Debbie told me I'd be setting a new precedent, but she never told me everyone would be mad at me for it. All the level-fivers were giving me snotty looks and saying mean stuff when I went backstage." In a singsong voice, Emily mimicked them. "'Who does she think she is—she's not even on pointe!' 'No one else got to pick a song with words.' 'It's way over two minutes.'" Emily's eyes narrowed with hatred. "You know what that witchy Pamela Barr said? The one in your grade you used to call Hershey? 'It was *my* idea first, but I knew Debbie wouldn't let me.' And then, after, when we had to watch them do their dances, I almost started crying, 'cause no one in my class would sit with me, not even Becky."

Screw them, Em. They're just jealous.

"Dress rehearsal's tomorrow night, and I don't even want to go now," she said as the tears started to fall.

You have to; you've worked too hard for this.

Emily looked across the room where she'd created a dance to a song she'd fallen in love with, and the full force of its rejection by her peers finally hit her. How many hours, Band-Aids, ice packs, Tylenol had it taken to make her solo as perfect as she could? How many bruises, blisters, muscle spasms, falls? And as she stared at the ballet barre, its wood stained with her sweat and polished smooth by her palms, the fortitude she'd needed to get through the pain and those dark moments of doubt slowly came back to her. Unlike some of the other soloists she'd watched tonight, whose "kiss-up" mothers did everything for them, she'd chosen her own music, had created her own dance, and had even thought up her costume all by herself. Rubbing the tears from her cheeks, she told her brother, "Screw 'em. I don't care what anybody thinks."

That's the spirit, Em.

"Takes a lot of courage to be different." That's what Esther told her the next morning, while they were sitting in the community room at Pleasant Oaks.

"That's probably what my parents would say." Emily turned her head slightly to inhale. Esther's sour breath was worse than usual.

"You didn't tell them?"

"It's supposed to be a surprise, remember?"

"Oh, yes; I forgot that." Esther tapped her temple with one of her twisted, knobby fingers. "I can remember I was baking blueberry muffins when I went into labor with William, but I couldn't tell you what I had for breakfast this morning to save my soul."

"From what you've told me about the food here," said Emily, "that's probably a good thing."

Esther's laughter sounded like the chirping of a baby bird. "You're right, Emmy, some things aren't worth remembering. So you forget all about what those girls said."

I never forget what people say, thought Emily, then, noticing that Esther was struggling to get something out of the pocket of her flowered housecoat, she asked, "Can I help you, Esther?"

"No, no, I have it," said Esther, her gnarled fingers emerging with a five-dollar bill. "I'm not sure what things cost these days, but this used to be a lot of money. So put it in a safe place, and when you go home, give it to your father."

"What for?" Emily asked, confused.

"To pay him for the tape he's going to make of your dance for me."

"He's not going to charge you for that, Esther. He was going to tape it anyway, and it doesn't cost anything to make a copy."

"Everything costs something," Esther told her. "Besides, I can't think of anything I'd rather buy than that. Why, I'm even going to have a party for all the old bats on my floor. We're going to watch it on the TV in here and have cookies and punch. Like I told Hattie, you're the best thing that's happened to me in a couple of decades. I'm so glad they gave me you instead of a boy."

Looking over at Howie Baines, who'd put his adoptive grandparent to sleep bragging about the A+ he'd gotten on his science project, Emily told Esther, "Me, too."

When her dad dropped her off at the high school that evening for dress rehearsal, it was Esther that Emily was thinking about as she walked nervously toward the building: "Takes a lot of courage to be different."

And that's what she kept repeating to herself as she strode down the shiny hallway of the new high school wearing her level-four costume, a garment bag slung over her left shoulder, the straps of her ballet bag firmly gripped in her right hand. Outside the auditorium doors, girls were grouped in excited clusters, talking and comparing their costumes, fixing one another's hair and makeup. Without a "hi" or a nod or a sideways glance, she glided right past them as if they weren't even there.

Like her father, Emily understood the value of words, had discovered their power in a poem she'd once written about black ice and snow. Strengthened by that line of Esther's, she cruised down the main aisle of the auditorium with just the slightest limp, her head held high, her eyes focused on the stage where she'd come to dance. To the pockets of girls of different ages and levels, who were sitting in the seats or sauntering about in their eye-catching costumes, she must have looked like someone on a mission. Even the giggling herd of level-ones in their cute little daisy outfits, who were chasing one another up the aisle for their last trip to the bathroom, broke stride long enough to go around her.

She sat down in the empty front row, and as she listened to the excited voices and banter behind her, her courage began to slip, the sight of the vacant seats beside her suddenly making her lonely enough to want to cry. She'd just taken off her sneakers and was about to put on her ballet slippers when she caught a glimpse of someone moving toward her at a fast clip. Glancing up, she saw it was Becky. She was carrying the same kind of garment bag as Emily.

As she unzipped the black bag, which was embossed with a pair of gold ballet slippers, Becky gushed, "I can't wait for you to see it. Jezum-crow, I'm so excited I can't even get it out!"

"You have to unsnap that button," Emily reminded her.

"Thanks. And, hey"—Becky put the task of freeing her costume on hold to look straight at Emily—"I'm really sorry about last night."

Relieved that Becky was talking to her again and that she would no longer have to sit by herself, Emily told her, "That's okay."

"No, it's not. I was a real jerk, 'cause your solo's so good and mine stinks."

"It doesn't stink," Emily told her. "It's wicked good."

"It's wicked bad awful, but who cares—I have a great costume." Then Becky held it up for Emily to look at. It was deep royal blue, and its silky long-sleeved leotard and wispy chiffon skirt were all one piece. "Isn't it da bomb?"

Splayed across the front of the V-neck leotard were thin lines of silver glitter whose pattern reminded Emily of water shooting out of a sprinkler. Reaching out to touch one of those delicate lines sparkling with light, Emily told her, "It's beautiful."

"It zips in the back." Becky turned the costume around so Emily could see.

"Sweet."

"Thanks. I caught my dad on a good day 'cause he had a big meeting he needed to get to. I don't even want to tell you how much it cost, but I'd be dying to know, too, so . . ." Placing a hand next to her mouth, Becky whispered, "A hundred and thirty dollars."

"Wow," said Emily, then thought about her own, which had cost next to nothing to make.

Carefully Becky began returning the costume to the garment bag. "Just wish my mom could see me in it. She loved this stuff, you know?"

Looking at her friend, whose mother had died of breast cancer when they were in second grade, Emily confessed, "Even though Jon never cared about this stuff, I wish he could be here, too."

"We can't think about them now," Becky told her, "or we'll both start bawling and ruin our makeup. Besides, looks like Debbie's getting ready to talk, so hurry up and show me your costume. I'm dying to know if mine's better." Becky gave her an impish grin and they both started laughing.

Rehearsal moved along a lot quicker and smoother than it had the night before. Getting to wear their costumes lent an element of excitement and urgency that made everyone take things more seriously. Even the little daisies seemed to understand that this was the last time they were going to get to practice and went through their dances with barely any pouting or tears. As her teacher liked to say, Emily's class had "shown up to dance," and Mindy got through the intro to *Four Seasons* with no problem and no excuses.

It might have been their teacher's stern reminder about respecting one another's work. Or it could have been guilt or loyalty or that they could tell Emily didn't seem to care what anybody thought, but most likely it was their intense dislike for the level-fivers that made the girls in Emily's class rally around her while she was frantically trying to change costumes for her solo. "Here are your tights." . . . "Quick, I need a bobby pin for her bun." . . . "Someone give me some eye glitter."

And when her dance was over, the things they were saying about her were quite different from their comments the night before: "She didn't even tell her mother about switching; how brave is that?" . . . "I heard she told Debbie she wouldn't dance to anything else." . . . "Those level-fivers are just mad 'cause we're the first class that ever had someone use vocals."

twenty-one

THE NEXT MORNING, Emily awoke to a hard rain—a ground-soaking, leaf-shaking, window-rattling rain. "Great," she told Sandy, who was hogging all the covers. "I ask God for a nice day and He gives me a hurricane." She could see it now. She'd be running through the high-school parking lot dodging puddles the size of Sebago Lake, her tights mud-splattered, her mint-green level-four costume ruined with rain, its delicate satin rosettes leaking pink dye like M&M's in a warm hand. And her mom would be racing right behind her with a platter of brownies for the refreshment table, yelling, "Couldn't you find a spot closer than the football field?" And her dad, who needed a wagon to lug all his camera and video equipment, would say something clever like, "Next time you can drive!" And right then, the hurricane wind that was strong enough to blow them to Oz would rip the hanger right out of her fingers, and the garment bag with her solo costume inside would fly away like a big black kite.

"I should have prayed to Grampa instead," Emily told her dog, who was now prancing and panting and wanting to go out.

You're up early.

"No church. No school. The only day of the week I can stay in bed, and Sandy wants to tinkle in a hurricane at five o'clock in the morning." Emily stared down at the trail of watery paw prints Sandy had left behind in her quest to sniff out Jon, then tried to step around them as she made her way to the couch, carrying her breakfast—a bagel and a glass of orange juice. After wrapping up in the afghan, she settled down on the couch, informing her brother, "It's really nasty out. Sounds like the safari ride at Storyland—you know, when you're waiting in line and the water starts raining on the tin roof?"

Yeah, it does.

Emily broke off a piece of her bagel and threw it to Sandy, who was soaking wet and begging in front of her. "Janey'd say, 'It's raining cats and dogs.'" She thought for a second, then shook her head. "I still don't get that saying. Doesn't make sense to me. I mean, raining cats and dogs—what's that all about?"

A figure of speech.

"Okay, Dad. Speaking of him, he's going to take me down to the Old Port this morning so I can get something for Mother's Day. And after that I have to go shopping with Mom to get the stuff for the party. I told you she invited Janey and Gram and

Dr. Radke to come over after the recital for shrimp and cake and stuff. I think Aunt May's coming, too."

What are you getting Mom for Mother's Day?

"I don't know; haven't had time to think about it. Dad's giving her a mother's ring; he had Cole's make it. That's why we're going shopping in the Old Port, so he can pick it up while we're there."

What's a mother's ring?

"A ring with your kids' birthstones in it. Nice idea, but I can't picture aquamarine and topaz together. I wish I were born in April or May; then I'd be a diamond or an emerald instead of pee-colored topaz. Whoever made up that birthstone list sure wasn't born in November."

Can you give Mom something for me?

"What? Macadamia nuts? You always used to give her those."

No, I don't want you to buy anything. Just say you had a dream about me and that I said to tell her I'm okay.

"Good idea. That'll make her feel good."

You promise you'll remember?

"I promise."

Swear to it.

"Swear on Sagey's grave."

A whimpering sound caught Emily's attention and she looked down at Sandy, who was stretched out on the floor and paddling her paws in her sleep. "Probably dreaming she's swimming in the ocean."

Nada. She's chasing seagulls.

"Make my bun nice and tight," Emily instructed her mother, who'd just finished brushing out Emily's hair and was now braiding it. "And no bumps."

"Have you seen my tie?" asked her father, rushing into the kitchen with a tripod and two camera bags.

"On the chair," said her mother. "And take the cupcakes out to the car before I forget them. And those two jugs of apple juice are for Debbie, too."

"What else needs to go out?" he asked.

Emily, who'd just been admiring the glittery coat of fresh polish on her fingernails, told him, "My solo costume and ballet bag."

"I'd better make two trips," mumbled her dad, then disappeared out the back door with his camera and video gear.

"Where'd the day go?" her mom wanted to know.

"We shopped, we cleaned, we baked," Emily reminded her.

"And we did an excellent job."

"Especially with the flowers," Emily agreed. "Janey will think she's in the wrong house."

Rushing into the kitchen for a second load, Emily's dad asked, "How are you guys doing?"

"We're telling each other how great we are," said her mother.

Picking up the silver platter of cupcakes that Emily and her mother had decorated with white frosting and tiny pink sugar ballet slippers, he said, "Well, can you do it in the car? We're supposed to be there in fifteen minutes."

"Take a chill pill," her mother told him. "And don't leave without us."

"Very funny," he said, but as he hurried back out the door Emily heard him laugh.

"He's more nervous than you are," her mother told her as she wrapped Emily's braid tightly into a bun. "You should have seen him the day your brother was born. He was halfway down the driveway before he realized I was still in the house."

"What about when I was born?"

"He hit every pothole on the way to the hospital."

"Is that why I was almost born in the elevator?"

Her mother laughed. "No, so don't go telling people that story. You were almost born in the elevator because you couldn't wait to get here." Her mother stepped away to examine Emily's hair from the front.

"How's it look?" asked Emily, gingerly patting her head. "Any bumps?"

"An eleven on a scale of ten."

"And my makeup?"

Her mother, who rarely wore any, and didn't have any on now, told her, "You did a much better job than I ever could have."

That's the truth, thought Emily, and then she quickly scanned the different lipsticks in her makeup case. After selecting Cinnamon-Rose, she climbed up on the chair she'd been sitting in and said, "Come here, Mom. This will be a good shade on you, and it'll only take me a second."

"It's pretty bad that I have to have my twelve-year-old daughter show me how to put on lipstick."

"That's okay," Emily told her, "you're good at other things. Now go like this, and hold still."

Bringing Sandy in from outside, her dad took one look at Emily putting lipstick on her mother and said, "There's a picture. Too bad my camera's in the car—where we should be right now."

"All I need's my coat and my pocketbook," Emily's mother assured him.

"I'll put Sandy in her crate," said Emily, getting down from the chair.

"No; I'll do that," her father told her. "I don't want you getting dog hair all over your costume."

"Thanks," she said, and then headed for the cellar door.

"Where are you going now?"

"Just want to see what I look like in the big mirror," Emily told him. "I'll only be a second; meet you in the car." Just before she closed the cellar door behind her, she heard her dad tell Sandy, "She looks fourteen with that makeup on; when the heck did that happen?"

Racing down the stairs, Emily thought to herself: Fourteen? Wonder if Nate would think so. When she got to the bottom of the steps, she headed straight for the mirror.

You look awesome, Em.

"I let Mom do my hair," she told her brother, and, turning her head one way and then the other, she was relieved to see there really weren't any bumps.

It looks nice.

"Thanks. I can only stay a half a second, 'cause Dad's having a hissy about being late. He's so nervous he forgot where he put his tie and will probably leave without us."

Mom's usually the one out in the car blowing the horn.

"Not today—she even told him to take a chill pill. What's he so nervous about anyway? I'm the one who has to dance in front of hundreds of people and Dr. Radke and Gram and Janey and Mom and Dad, who don't have a clue I changed my song."

They'll like it. No worries.

"Wish you could be there."

You don't need me—you'll be great. 'Sides, I'm always there for you.

Emily was about to say, "I know," when her mother yelled down the stairs. "Come on, Emily!"

"I'd better go."

Good luck! Love ya, Em.

Bolting for the steps, Emily yelled, "I'm coming, Mom!" She sprinted up the stairs and through the kitchen and was sitting in the back seat of the car before her mother even made it off the porch.

"All set?" asked her dad.

"Yeah," she panted, watching her mother slip into the front seat at last.

"How you doing, Ethel?" her father asked as he reached over and squeezed her mother's knee.

Emily watched her parents exchange smiles. She wasn't sure why her dad sometimes called her mother Ethel or why her mom called him Skippy, but they did.

"Better than you, Skippy," her mother now said, holding up his tie. "Found it on the chair."

Her father laughed, then put the car in gear, and as they drove down their three-hundred-foot driveway, past the Raccoon Tree and Sagey's grave, Emily could feel the butterflies in her stomach begin to flutter.

"How's my beautiful prima ballerina?" her dad asked, as he pulled out onto the main road and headed for the high school.

"More nervous than you," she told him.

Emily stood in the wings, peeking out at the auditorium to search the sea of faces for her parents. I bet they're reading the program, she thought, hoping to catch their reaction when they saw "Amazing Grace" next to her name instead of "Greensleeves" and "Jon" after "Dedicated to."

"Only quarter of seven," complained Becky, coming up behind her. "Hurry up to get here just to wait." She tapped Emily on the shoulder. "Can I borrow your lip gloss? I can't find mine."

Emily turned toward her friend and was about to say "Sure" when she remembered her makeup case was still sitting on the kitchen table. "You'll have to ask Mindy, I forgot my stuff at home."

Craning her neck, Becky said with both awe and fear, "There's hardly a seat left. No wonder no one in our class is doing a solo except for you and me and Tammy—what were we thinking?"

"I don't know," Emily told her. "I'm so nervous I feel like I'm going to puke."

"That's just what I want to hear," said Becky, backing up a little. "But at least we don't have to go until after our class dances."

Yeah, thought Emily, suddenly glad for her solo's placement

in the program even though it gave her little time to change. "Poor Tammy; hers is first."

An hour and twenty minutes later—after a cute little four-year-old ham in level one brought the house down with her stage presence and antics, after Tammy's solo, level two's performances of "Waltz of the Dolls" and "Rainbow Ballerinas," several level-five solos, two duets, a ten-minute intermission, and all three of Emily's class's dances—Emily remembered something else she'd forgotten in her hurry, besides her makeup case on the kitchen table.

She'd just completed her frantic costume change backstage and was trying to collect her composure when she felt a familiar chill on the back of her neck and got the slightest whiff of Consort hair gel.

"What's the matter?" asked Mindy, who'd just finished touching up Emily's eye glitter.

I left the cellar door open, thought Emily.

"Help me sit her down, Tammy! She's gonna faint."

Emily clung weakly to Mindy's arm, her legs feeling rubbery, her stomach knotted.

"Quick, get the trash can!" Miriam ordered, and somehow Colleen got it in front of Emily just in time.

"E-e-eww, I'm not good at this stuff, Tammy; you hold her," Mindy pleaded.

"She told me she was gonna puke," said Becky, running toward them half dressed.

Fanning the air with her program, Miriam, who was addicted to the TV show *ER*, barked, "Someone get some perfume, stat!"

"No way she can dance now," said Mindy sympathetically and from a safe distance. "Level five's first song's almost over."

Emily, who didn't have anything left to heave and was kneeling on the floor gripping the trash can with white-knuckled hands, slowly lifted her head. "I'm okay," she said, and though she couldn't hear her brother's voice, she knew he was there and what he was thinking: *That's the spirit, Em.*

It was enough to get her on her feet.

Emily blew her nose with a Kleenex that someone had handed her, then took a couple of deep breaths. Although she was clammy and still a little shaky, she suddenly felt quiet inside, almost calm. "I feel a lot better," she said.

Tammy, who always saw the glass half full, told her, "Least you didn't do it out there." She handed Emily a bottle of water. "You can keep it."

Emily took a small sip, just enough to dilute the bitter taste in her mouth, and a second later she heard applause erupt beyond the curtain like an announcement: You're next!

Becky, who still needed to get ready for her own solo but was reluctant to leave her friend, told her, "You don't have to do it, Emily; everyone will understand."

But even before the level-fivers came rushing backstage with flushed faces and eyes bright with excitement, Emily was waiting in the wings. As soon as the lights died, she darted through the dark toward the small glow-tape "X" in the center of the stage.

When the cone of white light shone down on her, Emily was holding her breath and a statue-still pose, trying to stare beyond the glare of the spotlight, certain she would see him, her brother's presence that strong.

A moment later, when the first melodic note sounded, she gave up her body to the a cappella voice and the powerful emotions provoked by its words and hers. "Amazing grace, how sweet the sound . . ." *of your laughter, your teasing, your voice in the videos.*

Gliding forward with delicate steps, eyes gazing past the light, hands elegantly reaching. *I'll never forget you handing me orange flowers, pushing me in my swing, holding my hand on a subway platform in New York City.*

Feet carrying her backward toward the spot where she'd started, right shoulder gently dropping, her reaching arms now arching toward her till they softly crisscrossed against her chest. *So when you're swimming through the clouds, Jon, don't forget me following you through the sumac, through the snow, through every race.*

"I once was lost. . . ." One arm unfolding to second position, body rotating into a turn—demi-plié—the soulful sound resonating through her, opening wounds. *Trick-or-treating without you, that empty hook on the mantel, your swimming medals in Mom's drawer.* Images propelling her across the stage, her piqué turns sharp, electric, white chiffon breathing in the breeze. Body straight but leaning forward, chin tucked against her chest, arms military rigid, hands clenching into fists. *Out at Calvary watching snow fall on a grave we never would have picked.*

"How precious did that grace appear . . ." *always there through the pain, the fear, the falls; your voice, your smell, your shadow on the wall* ". . . the hour I first believed" *I could keep you forever.*

But it feels like "we've been there ten thousand years" *and I'm tired of the lies and the pain and trying to be fine, of waiting for headlights to cross the poster on my bedroom wall.* Body bending with a graceful, fluid motion, arms sweeping, fingertips almost brushing the floor. *Still, I can't sleep, Jon, till everybody's safe.*

Face creased with grief, she halts before the curtain, letting her left foot take the full weight of a croisé-devant pose, fluttering eyelashes her only concession to the stabbing pain in her ankle. *Dad hiding in the Palace with his Molsons and signs; Mom on the phone again: I'm not coming home; and me practicing in the cellar, so afraid to be alone.*

Feet traveling forward—pas de chat. *Never getting to bury or see or touch you one last time; looking at a leg with rods and bolts and learning it was mine; Tiny Tim watching classmates in pointe shoes I'll never own; seeing diamonds in shattered glass, and my name in dust instead of stone.*

The anger, horror, devastation, and guilt all swirled into one as she soared airborne into a grand jeté en attitude, the landing solid, but out of reach of the spotlight.

For a heartbeat, she was left standing in the dark, but it was long enough to feel his parting touch as the words he'd said suddenly came back to her: *You don't need me—you'll be great.*

Her leg reached back for one last, slow turn, her right palm releasing a tender kiss as she said good-bye the only way she could. *I will remember you, my brother, my Jon, every day and all the time.*

The music ended, leaving Emily on the stage holding that final pose, her body open to the audience and arched slightly backward, arms high, framing her tear-swept face. The spotlight faded, disappeared, and then returned to allow a final bow to the brother she had danced for, and the audience she'd forgotten until the thunder of applause.

Emily waited backstage with ice on her ankle while the level-five class and the three remaining soloists performed. Although she could have sat in the row of seats out front with the other girls who were finished, she didn't have the energy or the will to move. She sat with her back against the wall and her left leg propped up on her ballet bag. With her eyes closed, she vaguely listened to the music, feeling so peaceful she could have fallen asleep.

The closing presentation was the usual—all the dancers onstage together for a final bow; Debbie thanking the lighting crew and her husband, who'd taken care of the sound system and music; the level-one moms who'd helped out; the audience for coming. Two level-five girls then presented Debbie with a dozen red roses and a gift certificate on behalf of all the classes.

When the recital was finally over, Janey was the first one Emily spotted as she carried her things down the steps of the stage. Limping through the crowd of parents and dancers, an ice pack secured to her ankle with a Velcro strap, she inched along in Janey's direction. So many people stopped her with compliments that it seemed to take her forever to make it to her family. Her mother was the first one to grab her, rocking her in a hug so tight it almost hurt. "That was *so* special, Em. Why didn't you tell us?"

"I wanted it to be a surprise."

Letting go, her mother smiled down at her. "Jon would have been so proud of you."

"I know he was," said Gram, who was still sitting in her seat because of her bad knees. "I could feel him right here next to me the whole time."

Emily leaned over and gave her grandmother a kiss. "Thanks for coming, Gram. Everybody loved my costume."

"You made me bawl like a baby, China Doll," said Janey, slipping her arm around Emily's shoulders and giving her a squeeze. "Jezum-crow, I still got the goose bumps."

Misty-eyed, her father handed her a bouquet of flowers, the writer suddenly at a loss for words. "Thanks, Dad," she told him as he kissed her on the forehead.

"My boys don't know what they missed," said Dr. Radke, giving Emily a flower sleeve containing a long-stemmed rose garnished with a fern and baby's breath. "You were amazing. *Really.* What a beautiful tribute to your brother."

"Thanks," Emily told her. "I'm glad you were here."

Debbie, who'd been milling through the crowd urging people to go out to the lobby for refreshments, placed a hand on Emily's shoulder. "You put that jump back in."

"I didn't plan to," Emily admitted. "It just sort of happened."

"Wasn't she incredible?" Debbie asked Emily's parents. "That's going to be a hard act to follow next year."

Emily, basking in all the love and attention, smiled thinly. There wasn't going to be a next year. She'd given up her dream of being a ballerina the night she'd faced the truth in the studio mirror—she had already decided her solo would be her farewell performance. But that was something she didn't need to tell them right now. She knew she'd have to break it to her parents gently, that the next time they cheered for her wouldn't be for her pirouettes on a stage, but for her butterfly in the pool.

"There's punch and lots of goodies in the lobby," Debbie was now saying. "I'll see you out there."

Although they had a ballerina cake and all that food back at the house, Emily wasn't in any hurry to leave. She knew Jon wasn't going to be in the cellar when she got home. By now, she figured, he was probably already up in heaven, pitching fastballs, because he'd once told her that was one of the things he missed the most. "I think it would be rude if we didn't stay for a little while," she told her mother. "Just for some punch? I'm really thirsty. Besides," she pointed out, "you need to get your platter back."

Her mother looked hesitantly at their guests; Janey, who'd given Gram a ride to the recital, immediately took charge. "Em's right, it would be rude if she didn't visit with her friends. Doc can follow me and Gram over to the house later. I got my key. I'll get the food out and the coffee going while we're waiting for you. And I'll take your stuff with me, China Doll, so you don't have to carry it around."

"Thanks," Emily told her.

"You sure you don't mind, Janey?" asked Emily's mother.

"If I minded I wouldn't offer," Janey answered, and everybody laughed.

"Well, don't leave yet," said Emily's dad. "I want to take some pictures first."

"And I want to get a family one of you three together, too," Janey told him, taking her camera out of her pocketbook.

When the picture taking was over, Emily's mother accompanied their guests out of the auditorium, and Emily waited behind with her dad as he folded up his tripod and put his video equipment away.

"Can we take the tape over to Esther tomorrow?" she asked him, sitting down in the seat to give her ankle a rest.

"It's Mother's Day," he reminded her, pulling the strap of one bag over his shoulder.

"So it'd be nice for someone to visit her, don't you think?"

"I think that's very thoughtful of you, Em." Then, looking toward the front of the auditorium, her father said, "So was what you did up there tonight."

Emily followed her father's stare. Dr. Radke had once told her during a session that when you lost someone you had to love them enough to let them go, and staring at the stage, now dark and empty, it was clear to her that she must have left that cellar door open on purpose. "You know what the last thing he ever said to me was, Dad?"

Her father looked back at her. "In the car?"

No, in the cellar. "He said, 'Love ya, Em.'"

"I'm really glad you have that to remember."

"Me, too."

"Need some help carrying some of that?" her mother asked, walking toward them.

"You can take that one," her father said, pointing at a camera bag. "It's not too heavy." Then he picked up the bag that was.

Her parents were ready and so was she; still Emily glanced toward the stage for one last look. Doesn't matter where we live now, she thought, he'll be safe with Grampa and Sagey. And with a feeling of relief, she got up out of her seat.

"How's your ankle, honey?" her mother asked.

Stepping into the aisle and in between her parents, Emily told them, "It'll be okay." Then she spread her arms apart so she could hold hands with both of them. After a shifting of camera bags, her dad took her left hand and her mom the right.

"We were so proud of you tonight, Em," her mother said as they started to walk up the aisle.

Smiling up at her mother, Emily decided not to wait until tomorrow to keep her promise. "You should hear the dream I had about Jon last night. . . ."